Unraveling

Book two of the Kirin Lane Series

By Kelley Griffin

https://www.KelleyGriffinAuthor.com

ASIN: B08952KH6W
ISBN: 9798651093014

Cover Art by Amor Paloma Designs, LLC
Edited by Wendy Waxmonsky

Produced in the United States of America

Griffin, Kelley
Unraveling, Book Two of the Kirin Lane Series

June 2020

Dedication

To my late Grandma Elaine. Thank you for being a trailblazer. For jumping in to become a reporter, photographer, writer, and formatter for your local paper when the men went off to war and for finding your passion for writing! You are the reason I started writing. And you did it all while taking care of your four young children! You helped to shape my belief that anything is possible. Thank you.

To my niece, Sarah. Thank you for believing in me.

Dear Reader,

Thank you for reading the second installment of the Kirin Lane story. Kirin grows even more in this adventure. She's challenged to hold her own in her ever-changing world. She still battles with trusting others but is learning how to rely on her own intuition and the people around her who love her.

Thank you for reading my stories and please connect with me! I'd love to know what you think of this book! Please consider taking a minute to leave a review. It's one of the best ways to encourage other readers to take a chance on a new author.

XO~
Kelley

Follow me on Facebook:
https://www.facebook.com/KelleyGriffinAuthor/
IG: https://www.instagram.com/kelleygriffinauthor
Goodreads:https://www.goodreads.com/author/list/991389.Kelley_Griffin
Amazon: https://www.amazon.com/Kelley-Griffin/e/
BookBub: https://www.bookbub.com/authors/kelley-griffin
Twitter: https://www.twitter.com/AuthorKTGriffin

Other titles by Kelley Griffin

Binding Circumstance
Entangling, Book One of the Kirin Lane Series
A Mind Unequal, Book One of the Casey King Series

Chapter One

For a woman who lived the first thirty-nine years of her uneventful life wishing for more excitement, Kirin Lane now begged for ordinary. It was the second time in less than a year, she thought she was dead. Obviously, she wasn't livin' right.

The first time, Saul Calamia—the leader of the crime ring who enslaved her father and killed her mother—pressed a desperate gun to her forehead. She'd prayed then for a quick end.

As if that hadn't jolted her enough, this time…she *felt* dead. Noise had ceased to exist. She lay face down on the cold, cafeteria floor of her employer, St. Mary's hospital. Shards of glass sparkled innocently next to her face like someone had sprinkled a sack of rock candy all around her. Vibrant rays of purples, reds and yellows reflected and bounced off the glass from sunlight filtering through the demolished wall next to her. It was terrifying and beautiful at the same time.

Black smoke hung in what was left of the hospital cafeteria, choking her like a dark cloud that refused to rise. She felt the pressure of a second blast, and closed her eyes, but still—no noise.

Nothing made sense. Her mind flashed images: the crisp fall day, the short drive to work and the smart, yellow scrubs she'd worn to instruct a fresh crop of incoming nurses. She remembered her jittering nerves dancing in her stomach in anticipation of today's lunch date. Today was the day she was to see Stacy, her BFF who'd abruptly ended their friendship the night Saul died in her back yard.

Their mutual friend, Laura had been the one to hatch a plan to put them in the same room to air things out. She'd invited Stacy to lunch in the cafeteria where they'd all once worked.

In the few short months since Saul's death, Stacy had become a recluse. She'd quit her nursing job, moved in with Todd—her new husband nobody particularly liked, who was also Saul's son—and cut all ties with some friends and family. And most especially Kirin. Gone was the audacious, southern, spitfire she'd loved since nursing school. Now, she was skittish, pimped out with Saul's money, and closed off.

The plan was for Kirin to grab food, waltz over and sit with them. Laura was positive they'd laugh and talk, like old times and pull Stacy out of her trance. The perfect plan. Except for one person who shouldn't have been there—Scar. He was Saul's brother and right-hand man. The undertaker of The Club. The same man who'd chased her in the airport and ransacked her house.

Kirin had snagged a chicken salad sandwich and a sweet tea and as she waited to pay, she caught sight of a familiar face with a scar running down one cheek. And panicked. His head snapped up at that exact second. Their eyes met. A smirk trickled across his lips. She'd been so nervous to see Stacy, she hadn't thought to check her surroundings first, like Sam and Stacy's FBI brother Steve, had cautioned her to always do.

Now, noise began to rumble in her ears. Every sound reverberated like loud whispers directly into her ears. Muffled screams, glass breaking, thuds that sounded like blocks falling on tile, car alarms—or maybe hospital alarms, she couldn't tell, all jumbled inside her ears.

She had to move. She was a nurse for Pete's sake. Trained in what to do in an emergency. She should get to her feet and help the others. But at that moment, she only wanted to close her eyes and let the dark overtake her. The scraped fingers on her left hand however, had other plans. They walked curiously toward one large piece of the blown-out window to touch it.

Squinting, she pulled her eyes into focus. Through the broken glass, a distorted wave of sandy brown hair covering a face came into view. The person's neck was coated in dust and blood. *Focus.* Kirin pushed off her toes and balanced her weight on her left elbow. Then she dug that elbow into the floor like an oar, barely registering the sharp glass cutting it and shifted her body forward. A few more inches and she'd be able to move the hair and see the face. Her right arm must've been broken or completely gone because it wasn't responding. And she couldn't turn her head to the right without unbearable pain shooting through her right shoulder.

With a low grunt of pain, she pushed off once more to align her good arm within reach of the hair. As her brain and eyes focused more, she realized this was a woman. With her fingers outstretched, she gently lifted the blood-soaked hair off the woman's face. Kirin's hand recoiled as if she'd touched a snake. A sob bubbled up in her throat right before everything went dark. One thought screamed in her subconscious as tears fell and she let the dark pull her under...

Laura. They got Laura.

Chapter Two

Kirin woke. Even before she could crack her eyes open, the antiseptic smell invaded her nose. Mixed in with it was the intoxicating, spicy scent of her fiancé, Sam. Her heart fluttered. Cracking open one eye she was inside a vaguely familiar hospital room. Her mind sputtered and flipped to make sense of her surroundings. The beeping of a heart monitor filled the air. Her head felt three sizes too big. She knew this room. This was *her* hospital. Second floor, ICU, overlooking the parking lot. She could tell by the direction the bed faced and the window.

A nurse she didn't recognize checked the monitor above her head. Slowly, she took inventory and tried moving body parts; toes wiggled, knees bent, hips moved, but ached, abs tightened hurt, left hand…taped like a mummy around her wrist with an IV sticking out. *Oh, God…did she have surgery?*

Her right arm was tied up in a sling and her fingers stung like tiny paper cuts covered them. She scraped her left thumb across the underside of her ring finger to check for her engagement ring, but it was gone. Her left eye must have been swollen shut. It wasn't responding, so she glanced around the room like a pirate.

After taking inventory of her bruised and battered body, she took a few deep breaths.

Her rugged man sat in a chair pulled up next to her hospital bed. The jeans she loved that usually hugged his rear, were crumpled and baggy like he'd lived in them for days. Sam's forehead rested on the bed with his face buried in his right hand. His left hand touched the blanket over her legs.

Without looking up, he whispered, "...please God. This is all my fault, please don't take it out on her. I'm the one that should be punished, not her. *Please...*"

Kirin tried to say his name, but some odd squeaky noise came out instead. Sam's head snapped up. She whispered, "Hi," and he stood, kissed her forehead, and wiped at red eyes.

Sam smiled down and whispered, "'bout time."

She tried to sit up, but both Sam and the nurse in the room told her no. Sam spoke, "They removed your spleen which ruptured after the explosion." Sam took a deep breath, "You need to lie still. You have a nasty concussion, a broken right arm and collarbone, a fairly good shiner on your left eye and some cuts and bruises all over, but you fared better than some..."

Sam's voice cracked as he trailed off. It broke her heart how tired he looked. As he glanced down he wiped at his eyes again.

Memories of the explosion played like a horror film in her mind. Tears filled her eyes. "Laura? Sam...Laura?"

Sam leaned in close and kissed her head again. "In a coma—still. She's been out for two days."

The tears that raced down her cheeks were a mixture of sadness, anger, and pure guilt. If she hadn't pushed to see Stacy, Laura wouldn't have been there. She wouldn't be fighting for her life in another room.

"I want to go see her *today*."

The newbie nurse she didn't recognize, let out a *"psh"* then stated very matter-of-factly that Kirin wouldn't be permitted to move for several more hours at the earliest. Kirin leveled a look at Sam. He read her perfectly, kissed her one more time on the forehead, ignored the nurse and walked out toward Kirin's boss's office. He'd get it done.

The nurse stomped out as Kirin's mind cleared and began churning. Why would anyone blow up a hospital cafeteria? What would Scar and Stacy gain by hurting so many people, especially Laura? And how could Stacy do this to her? Anger burned the dry lump in her throat. Holding back tears made her eyes sting.

Stacy was now her enemy.

The "why" bothered her more than anything. Stacy had acted friendly when Kirin strode up. She didn't even seem angry when Kirin scooted her over in the booth, so she couldn't escape, and they could talk. Stacy had grasped her hand under the table, firm, and spoke of friendship, but her face showed anger.

Her actions and words were in direct opposition of each other. It was as if she was acting—putting on a show for someone watching. Kirin's mind wandered back to minutes prior to the blast. She'd even hugged Kirin, then pushed her away as they stood to say goodbye. She'd whispered sorry into Kirin's ear. It didn't add up.

And then, when Stacy turned on her heels and stomped out to the waiting car, she hadn't looked back, but a mere second later, Kirin's phone had buzzed. A quick text that read, "get out." It was then, through the window she caught eyes with the man who shut Stacy's car door.

Scar. He smiled and mouthed the word, "BOOM."

Half a minute later the cafeteria exploded.

Had Stacy felt guilty that her "new family" had been responsible? Maybe. Maybe she'd meant for the warning text to go to Laura. She'd always gotten their numbers mixed when they were friends. Maybe she'd never know the truth.

The heat kicked on and the door to Kirin's hospital room creaked open a few inches. Sam's voice floated inside. He spoke low to another man with an even deeper voice—a voice she recognized but couldn't place, like a dream.

"Thanks again. How about 2:45? I'll grab the boys from school, get them settled then relieve you for the night, okay?" Sam's tone was almost a whisper, but thanks to the door opening and the acoustics in the old walls, she could hear most of what was said.

"No problem, brother. I'll go home, get a few hours of sleep and come back."

"Be safe. Watch your back." Sam called out as he placed one hand on the doorknob and walked backward into the room.

A giant bouquet of flowers blocked out Sam's face. He laid them down on the table under the flat screen. She watched him stuff the card in his pocket.

"Who are the flowers from?" She was wide awake and by the way he whipped around, he hadn't expected her to be.

"Hospital staff," he stammered. "The nurses and…your boss."

"Who were you talking to?"

He watched her, appearing confused by her question. "Who?" his voice sounded high and innocent.

"The man coming back at 2:45?"

"Honey, I think the fall did something to your hearing." A quick flash of a grin and he turned away. He was lying. But why?

She dropped it for the moment as one of her favorite lunch ladies delivered a tray to her room. Sam sprang into action. He moved the newspaper and a water bottle and placed them on the counter next to the sink. Then pushed the tray table over her bed and uncovered a cup of steaming broth and opened her milk like she was two.

He took great pleasure in feeding her. She'd argued she could do it left handed even with an IV in and tied to a pole, but it was no use. Sam made her laugh by holding the spoon out and making her reach for it and feeding her with airplane sounds. After she grabbed her incision site while laughing, he stopped.

After lunch, Doris—the head of nursing—came by to check on her. Sam took the opportunity to get out and stretch his legs.

Doris was, by far, the best boss she'd ever had. She was shrewd when she had to be, but fair and kind. And she'd back up a good nurse in a hot second. If you were you doing your job, she left you alone. She was white-headed and only a few years from retirement. They all dreaded the day she'd retire.

No sooner than Sam left, Doris remembered something she'd left at the nurse's station and ran back to get it. A bouquet of flowers. She set them near the window then plopped in the chair next to the bed. The woman never sat. She held Kirin's good hand. "I'm so happy you're awake. And I'm so sorry this happened to you."

"Thanks." Kirin thought about Laura. Doris wouldn't be having this conversation with her anytime soon. She raised her chin to fight back the tears, focusing instead on the flowers.

"Thanks for the flowers…both sets. You really didn't have to do that."

Doris looked around, confused and pointed at the ones closest to the window, "Those are from us…from my garden. The big ones look like they're from a delivery service."

"Oh…sorry. Sam told me they were from you… I probably heard him wrong." But her hackles were already raised. Why would he lie about flowers? She'd ask him about it when he returned. "Have you been to see Laura?"

"Yes," Doris lowered her eyes, "No change."

Nothing could stop the tears this time. Her innocent friend was lying in a coma. Doris squeezed her hand, "I hate to do this now, but I need to ask you a difficult question. You and Stacy were once close, right?"

Kirin nodded. Doris took a deep breath. "HR would have my ass for telling you this, so I didn't…" Eyebrows up, she looked pointedly at Kirin, who nodded back. "But she was in my office yesterday—*quitting*." Doris let that sentence linger before continuing, "But it almost seemed…"

"What?" Kirin asked, wiping tears from her eyes.

"She just kept apologizing…it was like she was *forced* to resign. She was so sad."

Kirin had gotten that same feeling before the blast. Like she didn't want to be the person she'd become.

Doris continued, "So, the rumor mill is telling me she was in the cafeteria before it exploded. With you and Laura. It's been suggested she was at least partially responsible for it." Doris watched Kirin's eyes.

She'd known Stacy a long time. Blowing up a cafeteria or being even partially responsible seemed so out of character. But, she had to admit, this new person Stacy had become...driven around with a bodyguard, dripping in diamonds, and fraternizing with mobsters—who knew? In her anger for Laura, who laid just a few rooms away in a coma, she wanted to say yes, Stacy caused this, but she couldn't throw Stacy under the bus when she had no proof. Involved with those who did the crime, yes ... but responsible for the blast, no. She couldn't imagine Stacy was the main player in the blast.

Kirin shook her head. "I don't believe that."

Doris stood and walked to the window, exhaling. "I just don't understand. Who would want to blow up a hospital where we help people?" Doris turned. "What kind of extremist would plan an attack on a place that offers healing?" Kirin watched her boss shaking her head, and yet all the while, knowing.

She knew what monster.

Well, in truth, *monsters*. She'd narrowed it down to two that might want her dead—Scar and Todd, Saul's son, who was also Stacy's new husband. One of the two had to be pulling the strings using what was left of Saul's money to get at her.

She was sure that both men wanted to make her pay for his death. One of these men had to be the ringleader enacting revenge for what happened in her backyard.

One thing was becoming clear—she needed to stop them both from hurting anyone else.

Chapter Three

Shortly after her boss left, pain meds were administered, and she drifted off to sleep. Those pills must have had magic qualities as they suppressed her regular nightmares. When she woke, the room was dark, and she was alone. The clock read 5:45 which meant Sam was still home getting the boys settled for the night.

She'd talked with the boys' nanny, Rosa over the phone right after lunch. Rosa had packed a bag and stayed at her house since the accident, so Sam could be with Kirin. They'd cried during the call, which was out of character for both. Neither showed that emotion often. Kirin hadn't processed how close she came to losing her life, until that phone call.

She rolled to the side and a shooting pain zinged through her shoulder. The buzzer was right next to her hand, so she pressed it. She wanted someone to take her to see Laura. Nobody answered. The hall outside was eerily quiet. Something didn't feel right. Her cell sat on the tray table which was pulled right next to the bed.

When she glanced over, it rang. Her entire body jumped. When she picked it up, the word "restricted" illuminated instead of a phone number, reminding her of the threatening texts she'd received when The Club had wanted the book. She answered, "Hello?"

"How ya feelin' honey?" The gruff voice dripped in sarcasm.

Her stomach twisted, and she instinctively tried to sit up straight, causing a host of painful stabs that told her not to. She could feel the blood draining out of her face.

The voice. It was Saul. But he was dead. Get a hold of yourself. It can't be him, Saul died... you saw his body.

She squared her shoulders and cleared her throat, "Who is this?"

"I think you know. But, for now, tell that fiancé of yours to stop meddling in my business or let's just say I'll give new meaning to your upcoming wedding vows of *'til death do us part."*

Her nightmares coming to life. Anger shot through her body like an explosion. The tight, menacing voice that came out of her, she no longer recognized.

"You will never touch him as long as I'm alive, do you hear me?" Her voice deep yet raised, she sounded like a protective mama bear. "When I get out of here—"

He interrupted, "Next time it'll be more than a few broken bones. You may think you've won…shut us down, but you're wrong. You in a lot of pain, honey?" He laughed a hearty laugh and it was then, her mind clicked. The voice was too deep, too southern and held an air of Louisiana in it. It wasn't Saul, but close. The inflections were the same. They had to be related.

Had to be Scar.

He continued, "You might want to find out who your future husband is keeping company with. Look out your window. Right now, he's got his arms around a dark-haired beauty." The phone went dead.

"Hello? Hello?" She yelled. Heat rose in her face, touching her ears. Sam had been acting strange lately. Late nights out chasing animals with his TWRA guys.

What if animals weren't the only thing he was chasing? Her stomach gripped and knotted with dread. She shook her head. She knew what she had to do. She'd have to drag herself to the window. See for herself. But what if it was a trap? Who knows, maybe they hired a sharpshooter to take her out. She'd get to the side and peek out.

Placing the phone on the swing table, she pushed her good fist into the mattress to help scoot her rear to the edge of the bed. Pain shot through her body. She concentrated on not using her right arm and not kinking her IV, because the latter would sound an alarm. Feet touching the floor, she took a deep breath.

Dizzy was a tiny concept compared to what her head was doing. Her thoughts were fuzzy as the room spun. She grabbed the IV pole for stability, but it wobbled as she dragged it toward the end of the bed. With each pull, it complained, squeaking out a noise she feared would get her caught.

Dread filled her mind. Not only would this journey be physically painful, but there was a possibility that if the caller was telling the truth, what she might see would break her.

One last push and she'd be at the foot of the bed. Her stylish, free-flowing hospital gown would show any sudden visitor her entire backside. But that wasn't the worst of her problems. Stabbing pain at her incision site felt like someone twisted a knife with each step. As a nurse, she knew that wasn't a good sign.

If she were gonna make it the last five feet to the window, she needed to do it before her body decided it couldn't take the pain and passed out. She sped up. The IV pole groaned and squeaked out it's dislike of this tactic. Hearing a noise, she froze and glanced back toward the door. She fully expected to get caught like a child stealing a brownie.

When she was positive nobody was coming to stop her, she took a deep breath and pushed her feet to continue. Her stitches pulled and tightened. She didn't care. She had to see for herself or it would always haunt her. The idea of the trust she'd built with Sam breaking, was enough to send fat tears pooling in her eyes. But she gritted her teeth and kept moving. She had to know if the malicious man on the phone was right.

In one not-so-graceful movement, her feet got tangled in her pole and her body pitched toward the floor. Releasing the pole, she caught herself with her good arm on the bed. Pain shot through her arm like lightning. The pole rocked back and forth until it finally righted itself.

She froze. If a nurse came in now, she could use the excuse she had to pee, and nobody answered her call, but she'd miss whatever was going on downstairs in the parking lot. She didn't care if someone walked in, she had to get to that window.

Her good hand grabbed the pole, but now her legs felt like Jell-O and her lunch began its journey back up to her throat for a reappearance. She fought the urge and pushed her legs to move forward the four more steps it would take to get to the window.

Doris's flowers glowed from the setting sun. If she lunged toward the windowsill, it should be wide enough to grasp it, but the flowers might suffer a quick demise.

Two more steps. Two more steps and she'd know if she'd made a terrible mistake by falling in love with Sam.

How much did she really know about him? Not enough if he had his arms around another woman.

One more step. The cold floor felt like ice on her feet. If she stretched out long enough, she could touch the window, but it'd be at the expense of her stitches. Her fingers clenched on her right hand as she gritted her teeth in pain.

Her vision blurred as she took the last step. She lunged toward the window, grabbing it and narrowly missing the flowers. She no longer cared if a gunman hid in the bushes to tag her. She'd almost welcome it.

Twilight had set in and the parking lot lights flickered to life. Neatly lined rows of colored cars looked like an ocean as far as the eye could see. Closely manicured and mulched flower beds lined the side of the building and ran along the sidewalk. Most of the leaves on the trees had turned their brilliant shades of oranges and reds and already fallen to the ground, giving her a mostly unimpeded view of the grounds.

Eyes wide, she searched the sidewalks. They stopped when the backside of a man in blue jeans and boots came into view. As she squinted to pull her vision into focus, a hot flash wracked the back of her neck. It was her body's defense against her pain. She white knuckled the marble windowsill but couldn't look away.

The man held hands with a tall woman parked illegally next to the curb, helping her into her car. Her long, dark hair and red lipstick stood out, as did her long legs and short skirt. As she slid with grace into the black convertible, the man closed her door. Something shiny on his wrist sparkled in the streetlight. The watch she'd given him for his birthday.

Sam. Her heart plummeted into her stomach. She fought to see through her tears. Sam must have made a joke because the wench threw her head back to laugh while Sam leaned into the car.

Her knees shook either from the weight of being on her feet just hours after surgery or with the realization that the man she loved was with another woman. A burning cry settled in her throat. She felt pathetic and pale, watching them. A part of her heart hardened.

She didn't need him. They'd been fine before he came along. He hadn't been a murderer in his old life of crime, but what if he was the manipulative womanizer Saul said he was?

Dark clouds formed in the corners of her vision. Her gag reflex was fighting itself not to throw up. Sam turned away from the woman, strutting toward the hospital. She must have said something because he stopped mid stride and turned back, jogging to her shiny, black car.

They exchanged words, he squatted next to her door and then they kissed—and not a quick friendly peck on the cheek—this was a full-on mouth on mouth, passionate kiss.

She wept.

She felt like she stood on the edge of a cliff, watching her dream die. The man she loved kissed another woman.

Enough.

Sam turned and jogged toward the hospital. Her vision went dark and her knees gave out. Like in a dream, she'd had enough wits about her to fall on her left side, so she didn't do more damage to her right. Especially since her already popped stitches were on her right side too. She must have hit her head on the way down, because all at once everything was silent and black.

Chapter Four

Waking from a dream, a bad dream she decided, was the worst. Her head throbbed. She heard faint, angry voices. Or maybe just one angry voice—Sam's. He yelled at the nurse or at her or someone, but she could only grasp bits and pieces of his words.

"…Don't you monitor your patients?" he spat angrily. "How could this happen? She was probably trying to reach the bathroom and couldn't get anyone to answer."

She heard him dismiss the nurse then walk right back out into the hallway and apologize. Kirin opened one eye. She was back in her hospital bed, lying almost flat with the covers tucked in tight all around to hold her in.

She shut her good eye while fine-tuning her hearing. Sam walked back in and sat on the side of her bed. His warm hand brushed back her hair. Talking to himself he said, "I should've been here. You wouldn't have fallen if I'd been here."

Sam stroked her hand. Hurt, anger and a desire to punch him in the face hit her all at once. It was the same betrayal she'd felt in the safe room when he told her he couldn't love and protect her at the same time. A disloyal tear spilled over, sprinting down her cheek. It must've caught his eye. He stood, holding tight to her hand.

"Honey, wake up." He pleaded, "open your eyes."

She blinked a few times, letting the light in slow.

He hugged her and blew out a breath. "Thank God. You okay? I need to get the doctor."

"I'm fine." She spat through tight lips.

Sam sat back on the bed, his grin turned down.

"What's wrong? You all right?"

"Fine," she repeated.

"You were crying when you came to…. Another nightmare?" Sam's brow furrowed. He'd mentioned a few weeks back, he thought her nightmares were about not trusting him, and it made him angry. He didn't wait for her answer, but abruptly changed tactics. "What were you doing walking across the room? Did you need something that you couldn't reach? I was only gone for a short while…"

She interrupted, "Where'd you go?" The question sounded far more accusing than she'd meant for it to.

He stammered, "…to grab something to eat. You were asleep, and I was tired of staring at these walls, so I left for a bit." His eyes shifted. "Why?"

Since when did he get so shitty at lying? Maybe he'd been that way all along and she'd been too deep in love to see it. She mulled over her plan. She wanted to scream and tell him she knew his secret and she'd seen the kiss, but something told her to bite her tongue. She desperately wanted to know more about this woman.

As soon as an image of the woman wrapped around her Sam entered her mind, her jaw tightened, and tears formed. How had they met? This woman couldn't be another client to protect since The Club had been disbanded months ago. But how long had she been in the dark?

She turned toward the window and answered so he couldn't see her eyes. "No reason."

Sam scooted closer to her. Then he wrapped warm hands around her face forcing her to look at him. "Kirin Lane—don't you ever scare me like that again. You know you're the love of my life and I can't live without you." Sam kissed her forehead and then scooped her up in an embrace. She cried silent tears.

Her mind had already begun making lists and planning how she and the boys would pick up their lives right where they were when they'd met Sam. He'd go his own way and never look back and that was simply fine with her. She didn't want to envision how negatively this would affect her boys, especially Will. She could already see the disappointment in his face when she told him Sam wouldn't be coming back.

She had to clear her mind as he held her for what, most likely, was the last time.

~*~

The next morning, a sea of people flowed in and out of her room. Doctors and nurses came in to ensure she hadn't injured herself further and to scold her for getting out of bed too soon. Her head pounded, and her body was sore, but other than that, she was more than ready to be released. The image of Sam and the woman ran through her mind, making her angrier and angrier. She wasn't going to be able to stay silent for much longer.

Sam was ultra-attentive. She couldn't even reach for something that he wasn't right there handling it. Guilt, she decided, was driving him now.

When the shift changed occurred right after lunch, Sam left to run errands and pick up the boys before bringing them up to see her. Her newbie nurse, Angie, seemed nervous taking care of her. She'd been told by the head of the hospital, that Kirin was her most important patient, and she was to tend to her every need. Kirin seized the opportunity of the new nurse's inexperience and convinced her to help with a visit to Laura's room.

Angie loaded Kirin up in the wheelchair, along with her IV, and they traveled down the back deserted hallways, unseen. Kirin was wrapped up tight in a blanket. Laura's husband Adam sat on a bench outside her room while nurses inside changed out her fluids, her clothing, and her sheets. He looked terrible. His face was ashen, and his puffy, red eyes told her he'd been by her side every second.

Adam glanced up and looked horrified when he saw her. She'd forgotten how awful she must look. Adam rose and walked toward her.

"Kirin." He said wearily, "Good God. Look what they did to you. I'm so sorry dear." Adam said, hugging her gently.

"I'm all right." She said, knowing she was far from it. "How is she?"

Adam looked down at his hands, "Same."

"She hasn't woken up at all?" Her tone sounded small.

"No. I had hoped that my voice, or the kids' voices, would trigger something, but I'm told it doesn't work that way. Her brain is still swollen from the blast. The docs think both of you flew back around fifteen feet or so from the windows in the blast. She just happened to land on her head."

Adam looked around to see if the nurses were listening and whispered conspiratorially, "She flutters her eyes when I talk. It's like she understands whatever I am babbling about, but she doesn't open her eyes or speak. But they don't believe me." He thumbed back toward the nurses. When his voice cracked at the end, she reached out and grabbed his hand.

"They'll do everything in their power to help her, Adam."

He stared at her like he was trying hard to believe her words. She squeezed his hand and added, "She's family—one of *their own*—and they'll fight for her, don't you worry. Only the best docs will be on her case and they'll go the extra mile and turn every stone to find out why she's still unresponsive."

Adam sighed, "I know. They've done so much already. Sam has been amazing. He's been in here a bunch...carted off flowers that some wacko sent and even had some of his TWRA guys standing outside just as an extra precaution."

"Wait...what? What flowers?" Adam continued to talk, not catching on to the fact that Sam had shared none of this with her.

"Oh, just some weirdo sent us flowers with some odd message on the inside. You'll have to get Sam to tell you about it. He'd remember what it said." Adam ran his hands through his hair and shook his head, "My mind is fried."

Two familiar nurses came out of the room and spotted Kirin. She recognized them from the halls. They hugged her and eyeballed Angie as if to say, "Why is this patient out of bed?" But her nurse just smiled naively.

Angie wheeled Kirin into Laura's room then excused herself to go back and check on some pain meds that were overdue. Adam followed Kirin into the room. It felt like a funeral. The only noise was the beeping of her heart monitor.

She was shocked how much her friend had changed in a few short days. She looked older and her skin was pasty white instead of her normal rosy-pink color. Her face was sunken in like she'd already lost ten pounds. Ironic. Laura would find that funny.

She was hooked up to a breathing machine and cords ran off her body like spaghetti noodles everywhere. Adam walked up behind Kirin's wheelchair and pushed it close enough to her side, so she could grab Laura's hand. Then he ducked out to give them time together. A tight lump formed in her throat. She'd be speaking to Laura without hearing an answer. Without hearing that soothing voice. She took a deep breath through her tears and began, feeling uneasy.

"Hey there friend...I'm so sorry... for everything. I *will* find out who did this to us and make them pay, I swear it. Laura? Honey, you need to open your eyes. I look like I've been in a fight and lost. You don't want to miss this face all battered up. Wake up." She held Laura's hand and smiled as if she could see.

Kirin had never cried this much in her life. She wondered if her tear ducts would dry up at some point. Other than Stacy not speaking to her, Kirin's life had been going along smoothly. Now, her best friend lay helpless in a coma— possibly at the hands of her other best friend, her fiancé was kissing another woman and her face looked like someone used it for a punching bag.

Laura's eyes fluttered and just like Adam had thought, it felt as if she could hear. Kirin began to ramble. "You remember our girls' trip about a year after Jack died? Remember you and Stacy thought I was depressed after Cancer took him so you two conjured up a road trip and called it, "Thelma, Louise and Louise?" Kirin giggled at the memory.

"We drove all over the Southeast sightseeing and laughing at ourselves. It was a wine-drinking, shopping, giggling, slumber party on wheels. We had so much fun. Remember we stopped in that little gift shop in downtown Atlanta and that woman behind the counter asked us if we were sisters?" Kirin laughed and stared down at her hands.

"Oh, remember that good looking waiter down in New Orleans with the Louisiana accent that we all fawned over? That was such a great trip. We laughed ourselves silly and Stacy... Stacy was so happy, remember?" Kirin exhaled, deeply.

"You're my sister, and my rock." She sniffed and continued, "And I just need for you to wake up." Kirin squeezed her hand. Nothing. No response except the fluttering of her eyes. She bowed her head and prayed the prayer she didn't want to pray.

Lord, let Your will be done. But, if it is in Your will, please let her be okay.

Her shoulder ached and the stitches on her side stung and pulled. She shouldn't be sitting up and she knew it. She felt a tinge of guilt for talking Angie into taking her. She'd step up and take the blame if they came down on her.

She was getting tired and knew Angie would be back to get her any minute. She tried to release Laura's hand when it dawned on her—Laura gripped her hand, not the other way around. A huge grin unfolded on Kirin's face as she bent and kissed the back of her friend's hand. This had to be a good sign. She'd ask the doc later when he came to her room.

Angie wheeled Kirin back to her room. She'd cleaned and changed it while Kirin sat with Laura. Now, she helped a worn-out Kirin back into bed where sleep overtook her.

When she woke, it was late afternoon. Her new nurse took out the IV and helped her into the shower. Her reflection made her gasp. *Sheesh.* She looked like a cast member from The Walking Dead. Her hair matted to her head and her face was swollen like she'd just had a four-hour face lift. Blue bruises lined her cheeks, and with bags under her eyes, she looked ten years older. Red streaks ran through the whites of her eyes.

With some worries washed down the drain, she brushed out her hair and put lotion on her face. She even put on lipstick to give her face some color, which felt odd.

Even though it'd been a few days since the blast, Rosa and the boys would still be shocked by her appearance. Stepping into clothes was more painful than the shower, but she felt more like herself. The boys would find it easier to see her in her normal clothes. Her side and arm were still causing her pain, but she sat upright at the small table instead of lying on the bed. She watched the door waiting to see her boys run through, which is something she couldn't have done just the day before.

The sound of little voices wafted down the hall and floated toward her room. Will and Little Jack were there, and her heart swelled. She hoped that the sight of her wouldn't scare them too much.

Sam made the boys wait in the hall as he entered the room first to make sure she was ready. He poked his head in and glanced toward the bed. Seeing it empty his face turned white. He pushed open the door and scanned the room. Their eyes met, and his face lit up.

"Wow." Sam said, standing just inside the door. "You look so much better." He smiled a broad, loving smile. Her heart had always leapt at such a smile, but she noticed it was silent. How much damage had been done by seeing him with the long-legged woman?

Sam shot her a puzzled look, then added, "Not that just taking a shower is that much of an improvement, but your whole demeanor has changed. You seem so much stronger than even this morning."

She was stronger, but not how he thought. She smiled. It was forced but he didn't seem to notice.

"I'll get them," he said, "they're beyond ready to see you. I've warned them to go easy and that you might look a little different, but you really don't look bad at all."

Sam strolled over and kissed her on the head, then ran back to the door and opened it. Will held his little brother's hand and they crept in, looking around like someone might jump out. Rosa had her hands on their backs ushering them inside. Will carried flowers while Little Jack held handmade cards and coloring pages. They walked shoulder to shoulder looking terrified. Little Jack caught eyes with his mama and his feet betrayed him as he ran toward her. Sam caught him and made him walk. When he was close enough she reached out, grabbed him with her good arm and pulled him to her chest. She didn't care if it hurt.

"Can you come home now?" Little Jack whispered. "Are you better?"

"Very soon, pumpkin." She whispered and kissed his hair.

Kirin glanced up. Will stood stock still by the door, eyebrows knitted together. He wasn't buying the story that she was fine. He glanced from bruise to bruise on her face. She caught eyes with him and tilted her head. "Will...come here, son." she commanded, but he wouldn't move.

"Will?" He glared. Kirin looked to Rosa who shrugged in confusion. "Son, what is it?" She let go of Little Jack and now everyone in the room stared at Will. This teenage angry voice came out of her oldest boy.

"Who did this to you?"

Sam answered, "Will, we've been over this. Strangers did this. They didn't mean to do any harm specifically to your mom or to Laura, they just happened to be in the wrong place at the wrong time." Will wasn't budging, and his eyes never left Kirin's as if Sam hadn't even spoken.

Sam mumbled something angrily, when Kirin interrupted, "Honey I don't know who, but trust me—I plan to find out."

Will's face softened. As perceptive as her oldest had always been, he might know something she didn't.

"Please?" She held out her arms. Will set the flowers on her tray table and ran toward her, stopping just short of her arms, then sliding in. He hugged her gingerly. She watched his neck splotch and felt his tears. "It's gonna be okay. I'm coming home in a few days."

Rosa stood close to the door and blew her nose. Kirin smiled and cocked one eyebrow as if to say, "Crying?" Rosa waved her off with the tissue and turned her head away.

After a quick round of twenty questions about every gadget in the room and a rundown about the food and the TV stations, Sam took the boys home, while Rosa ran to her house to pick up more clothes. She kissed her boys and hugged Rosa tight. When Sam leaned in for a kiss, it felt awkward. He looked at her with questions in his eyes. He felt it too. She needed everyone to leave them alone, so she could end things. A lump grew in her throat.

Rosa ushered the boys toward the elevator and Sam stopped at the doorway. He turned and watched her for a moment. A curious look spread across his face.

"Will you be awake when I come back?" he asked softly.

"If not, wake me up so we can talk."

He nodded, then looked at the ground and walked away.

When she was sure they were gone, she stood and grabbed her water. It was empty, and she didn't want to bother the nurses. She'd need it later for what would be an exhausting talk with Sam when he returned. Part of her was glad it was almost over, so she could stop obsessing over it, but the other part wanted to drag this out. She didn't want to feel the heartache when he admitted he was having an affair.

She held onto the wall and strolled slow and cautious out of the room toward the kitchenette. She'd been dizzy while the boys were in her room, but played it off well, she thought.

As she turned the corner, she noticed several things she hadn't when Angie wheeled her back. First, there was a metal chair posted up to the left of the door. They'd turned right to see Laura and she must've been tired on her way back and didn't notice it. Second, right behind the chair, taped to the wall was a handwritten note in Sam's scrolling handwriting. It read:

Brother's, thank you for joining me in this fight. Nobody gets past here. Please protect my family. I owe you.
Brothers 'til the end~ Pat

She had to read it twice. Brothers? Sam had only one brother, Seth and he lived in another state. Could this be his TWRA guys? That didn't make sense. He described them all as old and looking toward retirement.

Out of the corner of her eye, she saw movement and froze. An older nurse at the far end of the hall with a sour face scoured a chart. Her body faced Kirin, but her head was down. The nurse hadn't spotted the wayward patient in the hall yet, but if she looked up, there was no way she could miss her.

If she was going to succeed, she needed to move faster. It seemed like a tiny accomplishment to grab some ice and water by herself, but she knew it'd make her feel stronger and not so dependent. Something she desperately craved right now.

She was only a few short feet from the break room when she heard the low growl of a disagreement. She turned. Two men stood a few feet away, toe to toe. Their body language told her they were not friends. Bits and pieces of their argument floated down the hall.

"I don't care who you are," the man facing away spat, "my orders say nobody visits her unless they're on the list."

Then, she heard a voice she'd know anywhere.

"I understand your orders. I'm not here on business. She's a friend. I'm sure if you called Sam, he'd agree. You can even stay in the room, but I *will* see her today."

She grabbed on to the door frame. "Steve?" She called down the hall as loud as she could.

His face lit up and he sidestepped the man at the elevator, jogging smugly past him toward Kirin. His face changed from triumphant to concern before he reached her.

Steve looked like a tall, clean-cut, military cadet out for a run. He wore navy sweats from head to toe and running shoes.

He was handsome, but too focused on his job to ever settle down.

"What are you doin' outta bed, stubborn?" Steve chided as he carefully wrapped an arm around her.

"Just getting some water, what're you doing here?"

"Checking on you. Somebody had to make sure you weren't rotting away in this hospital." He stared down at her with something new in his eyes. Protective. He leaned her against the wall, took her cup and filled it with ice and water. "Plus, the way trouble finds you, if I stay close, I'm sure to see some action." His eyebrows danced as Kirin swatted at him playfully.

Steve had texted her several times in the past six months since Saul took his life in her yard. His sister Stacy stopped speaking to him just like she'd stopped speaking to Kirin. They'd bonded over their shared misery.

The sour nurse walked by, took one look at Kirin, placed her hands on her hips and said, "You aren't supposed to be out of bed."

"I'm not. I'm a figment of your imagination and besides, I have help." The nurse glanced over at Steve. He shot her a grin and her attitude softened. Steve had some swagger of his own.

The nurse looked back at Kirin, "Well, since you have *help* I'll let it go this time, but don't let me catch you out here again."

"Yes Ma'am," Steve answered as she walked away.

As they ambled back to the room with Steve's arm wrapped around her, she heard him smirk.

"What?"

"You. You're getting too skinny. I could about wrap my arms around you twice."

"It's the good food here, of course." She said wearily. "I remember now why I pack my lunch every day."

They turned the corner into her room. Steve helped her slowly climb into bed. Movement at the door caught her eye. The man who argued with Steve pushed the door open as wide as it would go and re-positioned his chair, so he could see straight into her room. He never offered to introduce himself or even smile. He just stared at them.

Steve rolled his eyes, making her smile. Then pushed the tray table so it hovered over Kirin's lap. He sat in Sam's chair and pulled a fresh deck of cards out of his back pocket. He and Stacy were both big card players and she knew, this was Steve's way of saying he missed his sister.

He talked and shuffled simultaneously. "So ... truth, how are you?"

"I'm ok." She lied.

Steve shuffled without looking at the cards and held her gaze for a few seconds as if he tried to read her mind.

"Um hm," he said, hitching an eyebrow.

"Really," she continued, "My wounds are healing, bruises are going away, stitches will dissolve, and the brace will come off my arm soon. Doc may even release me in the next few days."

"I didn't mean physically." His eyes bored into hers as he dealt.

She grabbed her cards and stared at them, not really focusing. Her life was going down the toilet. How did he know? As hard as the FBI had made him, there was always something real and caring about Steve. He wasn't stuck on himself with all his accomplishments. He genuinely cared about other people.

She'd sensed late one night that Steve's texts had a hint of flirty banter to them. Maybe he was just being kind or maybe he missed his sister. Either way, he was too nice of a guy to ever lead on.

She wanted to tell him about Sam and the dark headed woman outside but knew it would only muddy the waters, even though it was over between her and Sam. Admitting that, even in her mind, stung. She didn't want it to be over. And, if she was being honest, she still loved Sam. But thanks to her father leaving her, it'd taken so long to finally trust a man. And now, that man had broken her trust.

Steve's phone rang and he held up one finger but stayed seated.

"Withrow here. Tell me good news..." He paused. The crease between his eyebrows deepened. "How many girls?...Holy shit. That's a shipment. Thank our informant and get—" Steve glanced up and locked eyes with Kirin for a split second, then looked away, "... our interpreter ready. Yes, and notify the shelter. I'll be right there."

Steve hung up and grabbed his cards, not looking at Kirin. She stared until he glanced her way. His eyebrows shot up as if to say, 'your turn.' She pulled a card off the top of the deck and before she could ask what the call was about, he brought up Stacy.

"So, you know what's got me so perplexed?" he began, "You said Stacy held your hand under the cafeteria table and squeezed it, like a friend. And even the inflection in her voice was kind, but her face was scrunched up and angry, right?" Kirin nodded as she discarded.

Steve blew out a breath, "I think she was acting. For the benefit of the people who could see her through the window. So they knew her loyalty was to them and not you." Steve picked a card off the pile, laid down triple threes and slapped down a card on the discard pile.

It made sense. Stacy had hugged her, then pushed her away. At the time Kirin thought she'd lost her mind, but if she was putting on a show, she did a damn good job.

"Do you believe she's capable of blowing up the cafeteria?" Kirin asked, watching him as she picked another card.

"Do you?" he stilled, his voice tight.

"No. But, I think she knew something was gonna happen."

He nodded, "I think she's trapped inside their world. I've got agents watching her every move so when she's ready to get out, she can." Steve stared at his hand. "I'm sorry you were hurt, and Laura is in a coma. We'll pinpoint exactly who's behind this and bring them to justice."

"Scar," she said out loud.

"Who?"

"I don't know his real name, but he was Saul's right hand man. He has a scar running down his right cheek. He mouthed the word "Boom" to me right before the first blast."

Steve's mouth hung open for a beat. He cleared his throat, "What makes you sure he's the leader?"

"He blames me for Saul's death. And he resembles Saul like they were related."

Steve took a long breath, "...Brothers. They were brothers."

She swallowed that for a minute. She was an only child, but she knew the loyalty inside most families. She'd be Scar's number one target. It was her fault Laura was dragged in the middle.

Steve stared off, then leveled a look at her. "It's not your fault. None of it."

She shook her head.

"And besides, I'm not sure he's smart enough to be running the show. I think there's someone else, someone craftier."

Steve's phone buzzed. "Shit." He rose quickly. "I gotta go."

"You just got here…"

Steve leaned over, kissed the top of her head, and pressed all the cards into her hand.

"Don't worry, I've snuck in here before and I'll do it again."

Steve smiled devilishly and with that he jogged out the door and to the right.

Chapter Five

Absentmindedly, she shuffled the cards and thought about what he'd said. Was Scar bright enough to be the leader? Maybe. He had the look and disposition of a ruthless leader. What about Todd? Was he strong enough to lead in Saul's absence? To rule over Scar?

If not, she had a new enemy. Someone who wanted her dead enough to blow up a hospital. And what shipment? He'd deviated from the phone call quickly, like he didn't want her to ask questions.

Her mind spun and unraveled like circles of curly ribbon falling to the floor. Kirin yawned big. She needed to check her own chart. Whatever medications she was on were making her sleepy.

Her heavy eyelids closed for only a second, or so she thought.

Several minutes passed when she woke to Sam stomping into the room after having spoken to the man outside. His face was tight and pink like he was angry, but his plastered smile tried to hide it.

"So, you had a visitor?" He tossed his jacket on the back of the chair Steve had just occupied. His voice was agitated and tight.

It only took a few seconds for all her drowsiness to seep out leaving anger and adrenaline in its wake.

"I did," She retorted, just as harsh, glaring right back at him.

"What did he tell you?" Sam said, watching her. He pulled the chair out and sat.

"The truth," she fired back, "which is more than I can say for you."

Sam looked stunned but kept his poker face. "Stories, Kirin, that's all they are—stories. We don't know for sure. So, I'm taking every precaution. I've got friends standing guard while I'm not here. They're supposed to keep you safe and keep everyone else out, but obviously, that's not working."

"Why do you believe you need to keep me in the dark to protect me?" Kirin pushed herself higher in the bed and crisscrossed her legs. She ignored the stab of pain in her side. "There will be a time, very soon Sam Neal when you won't be around. And unless you're honest with me, I won't be able to defend myself."

"Oh really? Where am I going?" he said sarcastically.

She sucked in a long breath. It was time. "I don't know, you tell me. Let's ask this question again and see if you tell me the truth this time. Where were you when I fell at the windowsill, Sam? Or maybe a better question is *who* were you with?"

His poker face failed him this time. Those handsome features and beautiful green eyes she'd once adored stared at her in disbelief. Since he didn't speak, she lowered her voice to a whisper and continued.

"I saw you. With her. I saw you with your lips wrapped around some whore. Some crazy man calls and says to look out the window, so I do and…"

Sam interrupted and stood. "What crazy man? Who called?"

"I don't know. All I know is he sounded like Saul."

Sam's face scrunched up with anger, but his body pitched forward in defeat. He straightened, took a few steps and stopped at the window, running his hands through his hair.

"Well, it begins," he said quietly to himself.

She glared at the back of his head, willing herself not to cry. She wanted to scream. Anger and resentment raced each other in circles in her mind. She'd prayed a silent prayer that it wasn't true. Hoped beyond hope that it was just a misunderstanding. It was like she was standing outside of herself watching it unfold.

When he offered no explanation, she once again pushed herself higher in the bed. Wincing a little she took a deep breath and asked the question she most wanted, and yet didn't want, to know.

"Who *is* she? And please … don't lie to me."

Still facing the window, he hesitated for a moment and then finally said, "My past. She's part of my past."

An ex-lover? Or someone he'd protected and fell in love with? Her heart was firmly waiting in her stomach. She'd have to push to get answers.

"So, you're having an affair with her?" Kirin asked, keeping her voice surprisingly even, except her breath hitched in her throat speaking the words. This was more painful than the blast would ever be.

He laughed, turning toward her and in an angry tone he shook his head saying, "Don't be ridiculous, Kirin. No."

She folded her good arm into the one in the sling, across her chest. Rage engulfed her. She wanted him and his lies to be gone. Hot anger threatened to spilled over the edge.

"I saw you!" She yelled, flailing her one good arm, "With her…touching her in a way that didn't suggest friendship. Kissing her deep and holding her hand way too long…laughing and jogging back toward her. Closing her door and leaning into the car. Are you telling me I dreamed it?" She didn't care that the entire floor was probably listening. Sam calmly walked over and shut the door, saying nothing in his defense.

Kirin continued, "Is that what you want? A long-legged, dark haired, convertible driving wench? Then go. *Please*. You lied about where you were, lied about the flowers and have probably lied about a dozen other things…I'm done." The tears betrayed her and fell.

Through her tears, she watched him. He turned to face her and walked to the foot of her bed. His face was tight and angry still, but his eyes held sadness. He shoved his hands in his pockets.

She was terrified he would walk around the bed and try to hug her, but even more terrified that he wouldn't. She felt betrayed, cheated on. She could feel these emotions as if they'd been painted on her. His silence spoke volumes. She assumed he didn't want her but didn't want to hurt her, either. In the silence between them, she gave up. She took her life mentally back to the time before he entered it.

Take his clothes and shoes out of her closet...his stupid, ugly recliner can go back to his cabin, his four-wheeler, his boots on the back porch, his coffee mugs and anything else that reminded her of him. She'd have to launder everything to get that intoxicating smell out of her sheets or she'd end up a hermit, doing nothing except lying in bed inhaling. She'd work more, maybe take the kids on a vacation and do more things with friends...

And then it hit her... One of her best friends *couldn't* speak and the other *wouldn't* speak. She wiped her eyes with her good hand.

"Do you love her?" Kirin asked, her voice cracking on the last word.

He watched her carefully. She searched his face for any emotion when he spoke of the other woman but saw none.

Very matter-of-factly he answered, "I thought I did once, a long time ago, but no. I cared about her—about what happened to her...but no, I didn't love her." He stared at her. His tired, pleading eyes meeting her hurt ones. She blinked the tears out of her eyes and looked away. She couldn't take it. Hot tears were set free, running down both cheeks, and she wrapped her good arm around herself. She felt stupid and vulnerable.

When she did, Sam walked back over and stood behind the chair. His white knuckles gripped the back of the chair like he was squeezing it to keep himself upright. He was too close. She shot him a look of warning, she did not want him closer, she'd explode.

His face turned hard and angry, yet sad. "You need to rest, Kirin."

"No! No, I don't," she yelled. She swallowed a lump and continued, "I think you need to leave."

Sam sat in the chair with a thud and leaned forward. Her entire body stiffened.

"Why?" he said incredulously.

She took a deep breath trying to convey the depths of her pain. "I don't want to be with someone who lies or *can't* tell me the truth. I don't trust you anymore." She watched him shrink back into the chair like he'd been slapped but continued. "The person you're supposed to love is sitting in a hospital bed and you're kissing another woman."

He winced, and his face turned red. Somehow his anger made her feel better.

She continued, "You refuse to tell me what you did in The Club... I don't know if you were a thug, a money man, a pimped-out prostitute or a hired killer. Your only excuse is that she's "from your past," which tells me nothing. I don't know if you had a physical relationship with her or even why you're meeting in a hospital parking lot. I feel like a fool. I'm hurt and angry and I want you to leave. I don't need your mob friends outside keeping me oblivious in here, while you're on the outside *doing whomever...*"

"Go away," she said quietly, turning away from him.

Sam stood so quick it caused his chair to squeal as it kicked back behind him.

"You can't be serious!" Sam balled up his fists. "Kirin, you want to end what we have based upon a chance encounter of walking a woman—an *acquaintance*—to her car? Do you know how ridiculous that sounds? Don't you love me? Do the last six months mean *nothing* to you?" He continued, pacing. "The kiss—was something I was forced to do—I know it sounds crazy to you, but it was to keep *you* safe. The voice on the other end of your phone call, did *exactly* what he set out to do. He put doubt in your mind about me."

Sam stepped toward her and placed both hands flat on the bed next to her. He leaned in close to her face, speaking softer but still just as passionately.

"Don't you think I get jealous when Steve calls you or texts you when I'm not home? Then he waits until I'm gone and runs up here to sit with you?"

Sam sat on the edge of the bed and grabbed her left hand before she could yank it away and pulling it to his mouth he kissed it. "Kirin, please, please don't do this." He whispered into her hand between kisses. "Don't give up on us. We're going to have to be strong to get through this...I can't lose you."

Sam sighed heavily, "I'll tell you anything you want to know—just don't leave me."

Before she could answer, the door swung open and one of the elderly kitchen ladies wheeled her dinner into the room, smiling.

Kirin wiped her eyes. The woman had to be in her seventies, with kind blue eyes and short grey hair. She moved with a slowness that made you want to help, but with a fierce grip that said she wouldn't want it. She had no idea she'd stepped in the middle of their quarrel.

Sam blinked then moved to get out of her way. She smiled at Kirin with kind eyes and tucked a piece of her short grey hair around her ear. Setting the food tray down, she struggled with raising the table above the bed. The little woman pushed, pulled and tugged but it wouldn't budge.

"I don't know what's wrong with this one. It must be broken." Sam stood and tried to help as well but the table wouldn't move.

"It's fine." Kirin's tone was as kind as her impatient mind could manage. "We can fix it later, don't worry."

The kitchen lady wasn't taking the hint. She was on a mission to find the problem. Sam squatted down under the tray table to see what the malfunction could be. He lifted the table and placed it on its side on the ground. The underside of the table was exposed.

Kirin and the woman spotted the problem at the same time. A small black box was fastened to the underneath at the point where the tabletop and the base came together. It caused the lowering mechanism to stick. Kirin reached over to touch it and pulled it off. It looked to be a transmitter of some type.

Sam snatched it out of her hands, red faced and angry he stomped toward the hallway, growling back over his shoulder he added, "It should work now."

The kind woman extended the table over Kirin's lap, then lifted the tray of food and placed it in front of Kirin.

"Wonder what that box was?" she said as she idly straightened up the covers around Kirin's feet.

"I don't know." Kirin answered honestly. *But she'd bet Sam knew.*

The grey headed woman patted Kirin's leg, then shuffled out the door. As soon as she cleared the door, Sam stomped back in with the man who'd argued with Steve hot on his heels. The two men methodically looked under every hard surface, sweeping the room for any more devices. Both men were silent. Kirin wondered if it'd been planted by the mob or someone else. Either way, someone had either been in her room while she was out, or while she was wide awake.

When the lookout man stomped back to his post, Sam slumped down hard in the chair and ran his hands through his hair again. He looked tired and defeated.

Sam took a deep breath and pointed toward her food. "I got a story—you gonna eat? I'm not doing this unless you eat."

She took the lid off her food, grabbed the warm buttered roll, and shoved a huge bite into her mouth.

The corners of his mouth crept up and he continued, "When I was sixteen, my father was a mechanic. We were poor. He worked long hours but had a dream of opening his own shop someday. One day, a prominent man drove up in a flashy Mercedes needing an on the spot repair. My father moved faster than I'd ever seen and fixed the car quickly, just as the man asked. The man hired my dad to help him with a *project* or two."

Sam stared off in the distance, "My dad was big and strong and..." Sam hesitated, "*intimidating.*"

"My mom wasn't a fan of this side job, but when the money started gushing in she conveniently forgot. He used my dad's size to intimidate others to get what he wanted. Then, the man turned his attention to me."

Sam shifted uncomfortably in his seat and his eyes popped up to hers, expectantly. She hadn't realized she held her breath and had forgotten to chew. She chewed and swallowed the bite then raised her fork and stabbed a giant bite of green beans. Sam's shoulders lowered, and he stared back at his knotted fingers.

He continued, "I was your typical outdoorsy sixteen-year-old boy; tanned skin, muscles starting to develop, looking more like a man than a kid.

"He didn't want me to be an intimidator like my dad, but the man had other plans for a me. I was a flirt in high school like my mom. The man wanted to take me out and buy me new clothes—a gift he'd said, for my father's allegiance.

"My mother flat out refused, but my father was easily influenced. Saul owned an old '67 Mustang and had it delivered to our door. It was the car of my father's dreams. He longed to restore it. The antique car was baby blue, hard top and fully restored except for the engine work, which my dad was itching to get cracking on.

"My father threw me the keys to his old pickup and told me to meet the man at the restaurant he owned." Sam sat back, crossed his legs, and gazed out the window.

Kirin grabbed a bite of potatoes and tried not to make a sound. He was in the zone and finally trusting her with facts about his life in the mob. Her heart was beating fast and loud. She was afraid he'd hear it and get distracted. She closed her eyes and concentrated on slow breaths. He began speaking again as if she wasn't in the room.

"When I got to the restaurant, there was a waitress about my age. A pretty girl with long dark hair and God, was she tall. Not taller than me, but still tall for a girl. She had dark eyes and flirted with all her tables. My father had instructed me to go in and order food. He'd even slipped me a $20 with the keys, and that never happened. The girl sauntered over, flashed me a smile and proceeded to tell me that "they" had us both by the balls.

"I'd never heard a girl talk like that. According to her, we'd both been recruited for the same job. She was family and I was an outsider, but Saul had seen the same skill set in both of us. We could both coerce and convince others using humor, wit, flirting or whatever it took to get what he wanted. Saul needed attractive, young, assertive people on his team to help convince others when strong arming them wouldn't work." Sam fidgeted in his chair.

"Naively, I thought it would be harmless flirting and getting paid. I was sixteen and she was fifteen. We agreed this was the greatest job and it sure beat waiting tables for her and working as a mechanic's assistant for me. We both got new clothes and started talking every day, she was just like talking to one of the guys. She was tough, and she smoked and cursed all the time.

"She'd already experienced things I hadn't. She was forceful and worldly, and although she could charm the pants right off anyone—there was this other side to her. She had an inhuman ability to argue just about any point and win. Everything was a mental contest with her, and she never conceded."

Kirin had long since stopped eating. Tears raced down her cheeks listening to Sam speak passionately about this girl who was obviously his first love.

She could see the signs. She'd seen enough Hallmark movies. The two of them were in love and had been separated by some unknown event and now, they'd found each other again. He was about to tell her that his love for this woman was still alive and strong. She put her good hand to her eyes as more tears fell.

Sam stopped his story and got quiet. "Kirin, look at me," he demanded.

When she didn't move, Sam stood and turned her face around to meet his. She jerked her head away, picked up a napkin off her tray and wiped her face. Then turned back toward him. Sam leaned down. His pleading green eyes inches from hers.

"I don't love her, okay? I'm only telling you this because her story intersects with mine and it'll help you understand."

She nodded, but only because the lump that formed in her throat was burning and speaking wouldn't have been feasible.

Sam sat and continued, quicker, "We joked all the time that she should've been an attorney with her love of arguing, but at sixteen you listen to the adults around you. We didn't fully understand at that point what we were signing up for, but the adults did. My mother never looked at me quite the same way…"

Sam's voice trailed off, causing Kirin to glance up and see the tears in his eyes, "At sixteen, I lost my virginity…*on assignment.*"

The realization hung in the air. He was paid to be nice to women, flirt and schmooze all the way up to sex if needed. His words came rushing back, *"I've been with other women, but I've never brought anyone back to my house and I've never been in love."*

"She's in town because…" he hesitated. "She owns a very successful law practice in Ohio and everyone she surrounds herself with is married with kids. They seem happy, which is something that's eluded her, her whole life."

He cleared his throat, "We made a pact as kids. If neither one of us was married by a certain age, we'd marry each other."

Kirin caught on quick and raised her voice, "She picks *now*, while I'm laid up in a hospital bed to come after you? What kind of woman is she? Kissing someone else's fiancé…"

And then it hit her. This woman may not even know he's engaged, or that Kirin exists. He could be telling her he's visiting his grandma or something.

As usual, with his ability to pinpoint her thoughts, he answered her unspoken question. "I told her about you…told her we're engaged. But she's stubborn and doesn't like to lose, so she came here today to meet you."

The woman wanted to size her up. Kirin made a mental note never to wear sweats ever again.

Although she knew more about him than she had, she was still just as angry. The memory of him kissing the dark headed wench replayed like a bad movie over and over in her mind. He still hadn't explained why he had to kiss her. That just seemed so personal. That kiss was etched into Kirin's memory so that whenever she closed her eyes, a vision of them entangled in each other's arms was all she could see. A bitter pinch of betrayal engulfed her. His face and demeanor returned to normal. He was finished talking about it. She knew that look. Conversation closed as if he'd swept the kiss under the rug. It didn't matter to him, but it mattered to her.

Sam picked up the empty fork on her tray and filled it with mashed potatoes holding them in front of her mouth.

"No, I'm done," she closed her eyes.

"You have to eat."

Her eyes flew open, "No, I'm finished with this. I'm tired of crying all the time. I can't get the picture of you kissing her out of my mind. I'd like for you to leave, please."

He dropped the fork on the plate, and it clanged to the floor. He bent to pick it up. "This is ridiculous! It was one kiss that meant absolutely nothing. It's a game with her and if I didn't play her game, her way, then…"

"Maybe a kiss is nothing to you, but it's very personal to me."

"Wait, is this because of what I just told you? What my job was? What I *am*?"

She watched the flash of hurt in his eyes. She could tell this bothered him more than anything. She couldn't confirm nor deny until she'd had time to think. Everything in her world seemed so wrong.

"I just need to be alone…to think. And you need to give me the space to think."

Sam's face turned bright red and his eyes shone with nothing except anger and sadness. He grabbed his jacket and stomped to the door. He hesitated but didn't turn around. "Kirin, I love you. Remember that."

Sam walked out and slammed the door behind him.

Chapter Six

She'd asked the hospital staff to request that the guard leave, and he complied.

According to Rosa, Sam had picked Will up for the last two days and taken him to school without a word. She dreaded telling them that he wouldn't be around anymore. But this was something she just couldn't seem to get her brain to let go of. Rosa gave her daily reports on how the boys were handling not having their mom home.

Sunday morning arrived, and she was finally cleared to leave. Her neighbor, Arthur, offered to come over and sit with Will and Little Jack, while Rosa picked her up.

She'd kept her emotions in check for two solid days. Shoved the sadness down by busying her mind. Since she'd experienced a concussion she wasn't supposed to read, or think, or even watch hours of mindless TV, so she slept. A lot.

And when the nurses weren't watching, she used paper and pen to rewrite goals for her life. All in the hopes of keeping her mind too busy to realize how bad her heart hurt. She'd have her breakdown at home. She couldn't wrap her mind around the idea that they were over just yet. But she damn sure had to try.

While her nurse printed off the release papers, she took one last outing and went to Laura's room. Adam had just left to visit the makeshift cafeteria, which consisted of a few rooms strung together, where they served food while the real cafeteria began the long process of cleaning and rebuilding.

Kirin pulled a chair to Laura's bedside. She was pale and much thinner than the last time she saw her, only a few days before. The beeping of her monitors was the only noise in the room. She held her friend's hand and cried. Oh, how she wanted to hear her voice and tell her how much she was missed. She needed to hear that sturdy voice of reason.

"Please wake up—please. Don't leave me." Kirin laid her head on Laura's bed and tried to hold it all in. Laura squeezed Kirin's hand as she'd done before. When she'd questioned her doc about it she was told it was only a reflex. She wasn't falling for that. Laura was coming back, she knew it. She had to be okay. Kirin kissed her on the cheek and ambled back to her room.

In the hallway, her phone buzzed with an incoming text from a blocked number that read: *"Kirin, it's Stacy. Can we talk?"*

She stopped mid-stride and read it again.

She typed out quick, *"About what? How you tried to kill me or how Laura is in a coma?"*

The three dots indicating she was typing came up, but her response seemed to take forever. Kirin walked into her room and dropped her cell next to her packed bag on the crumpled sheets.

Her phone buzzed, *"You have to believe me, I didn't know their plan, but when I heard it, I warned you."*

Kirin's fingers couldn't type fast enough, *"Yet you're still there with murderers who tried to kill your best friends?"*

Her reply pinged back, *"It's complicated."*

"What do you want?"

"Meet me." She typed.

"I haven't been released yet from the last time I met you and that didn't work out so well for me!"

Kirin chucked her phone back onto the bed as the shift nurse waltzed in with a stack of papers to sign. She signed them all, without reading a word, seething from the audacity of Stacy.

The nurse piped up, "You've got a ride home, right honey?"

"Yeah, she should be here shortly."

She—not he. *He* wouldn't be coming back. He hadn't texted in a few days and stopped calling shortly after she'd lashed out and called him a whore. She couldn't believe she'd said it. It was a selfish thing to do, but at that moment she wanted him to hurt as much as she did. She'd regretted it the instant it came out of her mouth.

The nurse filled in a few blanks and gave her a copy of the papers, then left to get the customary wheelchair.

She'd done this. She'd ended it and had nobody to blame but herself. Squeezing her eyes shut, she willed the tears not to fall. So, he'd kissed another woman. That couldn't be erased, but Sam had finally let her in and trusted her with his horrible secret he'd been keeping for so long. He'd feared she'd hate him for it and what does she do? Calls him a whore. She didn't blame him for cutting ties with her, she would've done the same thing.

When the wheelchair squeaked into the room, she looked up to see Steve pushing it. Involuntarily, she smiled.

"What in the world are you doing here?"

Steve crossed the room and hugged her as she rose from the bed.

"Why ma'am, I'm your orderly. I'm taking you to your ride downstairs."

His voice sounded like John Wayne and he struggled to keep a straight face. The nurse behind him shook her head. He'd used his charm and credentials to sneak in and sweet-talked the nurse into letting him take her downstairs.

Kirin smiled and grabbed her phone, bag and purse with her good arm then sat in the wheelchair. Steve crouched in front of her and situated her feet on the pegs like she was paralyzed. He smiled up at her, clearly enjoying this. Kirin shook her head.

"I could switch careers you know if you're going to keep putting yourself in danger. I might just see you more this way."

"Very funny." She felt like it was her first genuine smile in a week.

"Kirin," Steve began, "You really should eat more, this chair is too light." Steve pushed her down the hall and onto the elevator with the nurse close behind.

"Maybe you've just been working out?"

He leveled a look down at her as she glanced up.

The elevator doors opened on the main floor. Down the long hall and past the front doors, Rosa's car was parked out front. As Steve pushed the chair toward it, he slowed to a stop.

"Oh, boy." Steve said.

"What's wrong?" Kirin followed his gaze toward Rosa's car. From her seated vantage point, she couldn't see whatever it was Steve could.

"Well, that's my cue," he said and handed the wheelchair to the nurse. He bent down and kissed Kirin on the head.

"Where're you going?"

Steve smiled a cockeyed grin and replied, "I'm trying *not* to start a fight. Text ya later." And with that, he winked and darted down a side hallway.

She sat up as straight as she could and craned her neck.

Sam leaned against Rosa's car, arms crossed and glaring.

Chapter Seven

The nurse continued to push her without breaking stride. "Nice guy. Is he a relative?" She'd asked about Steve, but stared at Sam. The nurse knew Kirin was engaged. Kirin didn't respond. She was transfixed on Sam's angry face. She'd swear steam rose from the top of his head.

He pushed off Rosa's car and jogged to the sliding doors when they opened. His face had softened but only a little.

"Hey there," he said through gritted teeth, speaking more to the nurse than his ex-fiancé.

"Is this your ride, Ma'am?" The nurse bent down for her answer.

"I…I believe it is." She tried for cheerful.

Why was he here? Knowing Rosa, this was her idea to get them speaking again. She'd probably make up some excuse as to why she had to ask Sam to come instead of her.

Sam threw her bag into the back of Rosa's light grey Camry then helped her into the car. It was all for show. He wanted to look like the concerned ex-boyfriend to the nursing staff. When his door closed, and they were both buckled in, he started the car. The first few minutes of the drive were eerily quiet.

Sam cleared his throat and began, "How're you feeling?"

"Fine."

"Why haven't you returned my calls?"

"I don't know." She answered truthfully.

Truth was she missed him…ached for him even. The hole in her heart from not talking to him had reached crater size. She'd cried several times that first day, but only when nobody was around. She felt horrible for what she'd said. But in the end, she knew it was over.

Sam watched her, reached over, and grabbed her hand and brought it to his mouth. His warm breath on her skin sent chills spiraling up her arms.

"Kirin, I'm sorry…for everything. For you being in that cafeteria when it blew up, for lying about the flowers, for Laura and for kissing *her*. I know it doesn't make it right, but it was not done out of passion or love, only obligation."

Slow, Kirin turned toward him, fresh tears pooled inside the corners.

"Obligation? How?"

Sam took a breath but kept a tight grip on her hand.

"I need her as an ally right now. I don't know which Club operatives I can trust. She gives me information and I lead her on. I know it sounds cruel, but it's what we've always done. Normally, a little harmless flirting to get information out of her is easy, but she knows about you now and she's testing me to see how far I'll go to protect you." Sam grew silent and stared out at the cars in front of him.

She jerked her hand away. She understood perfectly. This woman wanted him for herself and planned to ruin their relationship to steal him. He'd play the wench's game all in the name of protecting her. She cut to the chase.

"So, you'll sleep with her to keep me safe—which will *end* us?"

Sam's head snapped toward her, then he jerked the wheel sending Rosa's car careening into the emergency lane. He stomped the brakes so hard her seatbelt bit into her shoulder. He threw the car in park and flung his seatbelt off, turning his body toward hers.

"Listen to me right now. I'm not a puppet and I'm not gonna sit by and let anyone come between us. I made a poor decision—*one*. It meant nothing to me. I was only trying to keep the information line open for you.

"It was my job. And this was how I operated before you. No feelings, just mostly harmless flirting. I even made friends once with an 85-year-old widow named Elaine. She had property Saul wanted. She knew what kind of character he had and wouldn't sell to him. We played checkers in her nursing home every few days. She gave me life lessons and I gave her company. No physical relationship there, but she eventually decided to sell to a broker who sold it to him. Everyone won. So, it wasn't *always* physical.

"But with Gianna…"

Kirin interrupted, "That's her name?"

"Yes. In Gianna's early days, for her, it was always physical. She'd lost her virginity at fourteen, way before I met her, and she's always used sex to get what she wanted."

Sam continued, pointing at Kirin. "Before you let your imagination run wild, no… *never* with her. But she did teach me how to wield people to get what I wanted."

Sam picked her hand back up, holding it between both of his hands. "I love you, Kirin and nothing that happens will change that fact."

Sam scooted his body closer and whispered, "Please forgive me—my life doesn't make sense without you."

Kirin glanced out the windshield. Trusting people had always been her biggest obstacle. She didn't know which way to go. On the one hand, his argument made sense, Gianna had inside information and she wanted him for herself, so he had to pretend to be interested…but kissing her? That just seemed so personal.

But, maybe in his world it wasn't. Maybe the act seemed more like a routine—like brushing his teeth or tying his shoes.

His kisses with her had always been passionate. That first time in the cabin— she shuddered at the memory. Misreading her, he switched on the heat. It wasn't the crisp October mountain air that caused her goosebumps.

Without warning, he pulled her into his arms, gently trying not to hurt her, but with enough force she couldn't wriggle free. The betrayal was still there but understanding that his frame of reference was so different from hers, it began to fade. After a moment, she melted into him, his familiar smell and warm arms wrapped around her and her whole body relaxed.

"I love you." Sam whispered into her hair.

She didn't return the sentiment…just couldn't yet. He cleared his throat.

She felt it but couldn't bring herself to say it. She'd say it later. They separated back into their own seats. Sam's phone buzzed. He looked at the number as if he didn't recognize it.

"Hello?" He barked. His face fell flat and ashen, then turned red in an instant. His eyes narrowed as he listened to the male voice she could barely hear. Sam pushed open the driver's side door to get out.

"You listen to me, you sorry son of a…." His door slammed as he walked around the back of the car. She unhooked her seat belt and lowered her window and inch to eavesdrop.

"You leave us alone and leave *her* alone—she's your family for Christ's sake! You know what she's been through and she's finally gotten her life back together. She doesn't want this. Leave her alone and let her go back where she came from. She isn't the one you want, we are." Sam listened.

"…Come after us, you piece of shit, I dare you. I have an arsenal waiting to unleash on you." Sam paused. "Oh, don't you worry about me, I'll be ready." He pushed the button and stomped back toward the driver's side window while she pressed the button to roll hers up. Sam jumped back into the car, put it in drive and they sped away in silence.

"Who was that?"

"Nobody important," the muscles in his jaw tightened.

She stared out the window. That call was about Gianna, not her. He must be trying desperately to save both her and Gianna. At some point she feared he'd have to choose.

"Kirin, I want you to promise me something."

"What?"

"Promise me you won't forget that you and only you are the love of my life. Everything I'll have to do in the coming weeks is to protect you and the boys. Even if my actions seem wrong to you, they're done with the best intentions. Promise me you'll remember, no matter what, okay?"

"I promise," she answered.

"Now, let's get you home, I know some small humans who can't wait to see you."

Chapter Eight

Rosa stared down at the sleeping girl's chubby cheeks. *Fifteen*. She was only a baby. And exactly how old she'd been when she was taken.

She glanced around the room. She couldn't save them all, but God how she wanted to. Her sister reminded her of this each week. But still she returned. She had to help. Had to try and stop the cycle. She'd been working with two other rebels to intercept the girls, nurse them back to health and reunite them with their families.

These naïve parents, wishing for a better life for their daughters, sold them into sex trafficking and slavery without even knowing it.

She could help with the translation, but also with the scars. The ones on the inside anyway. But now, with their regular nurse unable to help, she'd been working on the scars on the outside too.

With Kirin's father's help, she'd pulled herself out of the business at twenty-five. Ten years she'd been forced into slavery with these monsters.

And now, she had a family. *His* family. His grandchildren were like her own blood. She'd never put them in danger. She'd turned things around and made something of her life, but it seemed like a lifetime ago when he'd found her. He'd turned his own sadness and misfortune around and saved people like her, and like Sam.

She sure hoped Sam knew what he was doing.

For now, she'd have to continue working with her treacherous informant on the inside.

Her only goal was to keep her two worlds apart and get these girls to safety.

Chapter Nine

Kirin had been lost in thought when they reached her house, or she'd have seen the signs. She stared at the throngs of parked cars neatly lining both sides of her long driveway. She hadn't hit her head that hard in the blast, but for as long as it took her to catch on, anyone would have thought she had. Sam took her hand, kissed it, and chuckled at her confused expression.

"Party time," his eyebrows wriggled up and down.

So that's why Rosa didn't pick her up. She'd bet Rosa had been cooking for days for this sized crowd. As they pulled right up front, it looked like fifty people poured out of her house like ants, smiling and clapping.

Kirin's hand flew to her mouth. Happy tears this time, pooled in her eyes. She was overwhelmed. Sam parked Rosa's car and ran around to her side, beaming as he helped her out of the car and up the steps. Her whole family was there, Kathy, Dean, Maggie, Rosa, Arthur and even Steve stood on her porch holding a beer grinning at her. A few of Steve's FBI team in full gear stood off to one side, not celebrating, and looking uneasy. They must've been on duty. She recognized hospital nurses, doctors, and even some cafeteria workers, who hugged and patted her as she hobbled up the steps.

Her farmhouse was lit from within, with music playing from the back yard. Each room had a different welcome home sign. She could tell the ones that were made by her boys. Oregano and the delicious smell of Rosa's homemade lasagna and garlic bread wafted through the house.

Every person seemed to have a smile and a glass in their hand. Her study had been turned into a makeshift bar with wine, champagne, and beer. As she and Sam ambled toward the crowded kitchen, she spotted Rosa. Using the towel hung over her shoulder, she dabbed at one eye, then winked at Kirin before darting into the pantry.

Her focus turned toward the dining room and the most beautiful sight. Her boys sat at the table eating and coloring more signs. Aunt Kathy spotted her first and ran over to grab her in a fierce hug. Little Jack scrambled off his chair and raced Will to get to her. Ignoring the pain, she lifted them both. Sam was by her side in an instant, holding Will to lessen the weight. Maggie called to them from the other side of the room and snapped a quick family picture.

Just hours before, she'd imagined coming home to an empty house with Sam's things gone, sitting in a chair trying to put her life back together. Here, with all her friends, family and Sam by her side, this alternate ending had seemed impossible.

One of the docs from her hospital asked when she'd last taken her meds. When she responded first thing this morning, he placed a full wine glass in her hand. An hour later, her brain was tired, but her body was free of pain and relaxed. Walking from room to room greeting everyone, she noticed a few things in her house had changed.

First, Sam's hideous recliner was missing. She glanced around. Maybe they moved it to her bedroom to make room for the party? But then she ventured into her room and froze.

All his things were gone: clothes, boots, ties, razor, and toothbrush. A huge lump formed in her throat. He must've already had the party planned when their relationship hit a snag.

Kirin gulped her wine then ambled downstairs to find him. He was on the back porch in the dark, talking with Steve and a few others at the party. She watched through the door listening in on their conversation.

Steve smiled, raising his beer bottle. The other men followed and so did Sam. The clinks of the bottles hitting and men laughing caused her to strain to hear Steve's speech.

"Here's to today's success. We didn't get the big fish, but we secured *two tons* of his most prized powder, twelve girls and we've not had a single casualty in recent days. We'll get him. He'll screw up one of these times and we will toss his ass…"

As soon as her back door creaked, all noise ceased. They stared at her.

"What's goin' on, guys?" She eyeballed each one.

Sam stepped forward, kissing her cheek, "Hi honey." He added cheerfully.

"You guys plotting to take over the world, 'cause that's what it feels like out here."

"Yep… you caught us." Steve said dryly, "Good job junior-sleuth."

Kirin turned and leveled a look at him. "Fine, don't tell me. You know I'll end up right in the middle of it anyway. I always do."

Steve raised his beer bottle again and clinked it with Sam's. "Ain't that the truth."

She shook her head at Steve. He'd been a good friend to both she and Sam through everything. Sam started up a conversation about target shooting with one of the other FBI guys, so she took the opportunity to talk with Steve.

"She texted me," Kirin whispered, taking a sip of wine.

"She did?" he lowered his beer and moved closer. "What did she say?"

"That she didn't have anything to do with the blast. And once she found out about it, she tried to warn us. I asked her why she was still living with murderers and she said, 'It's complicated."

Steve looked like he could bite through a nail.

"Dammit… Todd has something over her head. She's not like this, you know. She won't even speak to my parents but every once in a while and only for a few minutes. They're keeping her there somehow… I think she knows I've got agents following her. One agent was hidden and took some surveillance pictures of her. She couldn't have seen him, but somehow she knew he was there. The last picture he took was of her shooting him a bird."

Steve grinned wide, then took a long pull on his beer. "That was our sign as kids. We flipped each other off behind our parents' backs all the time. So much so that when we became adults, we still did it all the time. For us, it's more like a "Hello." I think it's her way of communicating with me."

Steve sounded so sad. He took another swig of his beer. Then asked, "Did she say anything else?"

Kirin waffled whether to tell him Stacy wanted to meet. Knowing him, he'd have a swat team there and screw the whole thing up. She opted to lie.

"Not really," Kirin looked down at her wine. "I think she just wanted me to know that she didn't cause the blast."

Steve glared at her like he could see right through her. He always could.

"That's it? You're sure?"

"Want to see the text, detective?" Kirin challenged.

"No. I just hope you're smart enough not to go if she reaches out and wants to meet. And if you do go, I wouldn't go alone…they may have some sort of hold on her and she may put you in harm's way without realizing it."

Sam caught the last of that part of the conversation. Walking back over, he suddenly looked angry.

"You're not stupid enough to meet Stacy, are you?"

Sam's wide eyes indicated he'd clearly said this without thinking it through. Then he backed up, apparently realizing how harsh he'd sounded. "I mean, she could very well bait you…for them."

Steve was smart enough to back up a step, knowing that Sam had set her off.

Kirin set her jaw and leaned toward Sam, "No, I wouldn't be *stupid enough* to meet her, but I'll figure out a way to bring her back." Kirin pinned Sam with her eyes and added, "You're not the only one trying to protect more than one person."

She turned on her heels, chugged the last of her wine and let the backdoor slam behind her.

~*~

When the last guests had left, the little boys were in bed and Rosa had gone home, Sam and Kirin cleaned up from the party in total silence. She picked up all the paper plates and cups and threw them in the garbage while Sam finished the dishes. The wedge she felt between them seemed wide and cold. She was sure he felt it too. He watched her out of the corner of his eye.

Her pain meds had long since worn off, but her wine consumption had been keeping the pain at bay. That too was wearing off. Her side and arm both ached. They hadn't spoken to each other since the back porch.

"Where do these platters go?" he asked innocently.

"Pantry—I'll get them." She dropped a paper plate into the loose garbage bag and walked into the kitchen. Then picked the platters up with her good hand, one at a time, and carried them to the pantry placing them on the top shelf. By the third platter, her side began to ache, and her pain doubled.

She searched for her purse to take a pain pill when Sam pointed, "I already put two on the counter and there's a glass of water. I thought you'd need one before now, so I set it out a while ago." His eyes held love and kindness. Anticipating her needs was how Sam showed his love, no matter what argument they were in.

She thanked him, took the meds and drank the rest of the water, which ignited her wine-soaked brain causing a relapse of tipsy. She leaned up against the counter and watched him wash dishes, waiting for the feeling to pass. He was so careful with each dish, washing, rinsing and drying each one and being so meticulous handling each slippery plate with his careful hands. This was exactly how he treated her.

"Did you move all your things out?" She asked abruptly, stunning him. He froze in mid wiping of a plate and turned to face her.

"Yes."

"Why?" Her tone was more of a whine. She didn't even try to keep the hurt out of her voice.

"I think…it's best if we have this conversation later. Let's get the house back to normal and then we can…"

"No," She crossed her good arm, "Now. Why did you move your stuff out?"

Sam took a deep breath, "To show everyone *watching* that we're through."

"Why?"

Sam sighed and tossed the plate up in the cabinet. It clanged and settled, then he slammed the door.

"So *she* and everyone else will think that I picked her over you."

Kirin stared down at her floor. She'd kept the sadness at bay all night, hoping it was a mistake. That his things had just been moved for the party, but now the truth stabbed in her chest like a dagger.

"Go then. I'll finish up. It'll look like you changed your mind if you stay much longer."

Sam turned back around toward the sink, "No."

"It's 11 o'clock… you need to go *home*…" Her breath caught. She didn't want to know but had to ask. She cleared her throat.

"Will *she* be sleeping at your house?" The giant knot in her stomach tightened.

Sam spun around, red faced.

"Dammit Kirin, I thought you understood …" he yelled. "No, I won't be sleeping with her nor will I be doing anything else with her. She won't be spending any time at the cabin. It's just a show, that's it. I've looked forward to holding you in *our* bed in *our* house for two weeks and I'll be damned if I'm leaving.

"I'm staying here tonight, whether you like it or not."

Sam slammed the last cabinet door, threw the towel onto the counter, and walked menacingly toward her. She stepped back as he reached her, gently took her hand, turned off the lights and then led her upstairs.

Chapter Ten

When she woke the next morning, Sam was gone. She could feel his absence before she even opened her eyes. Too afraid to hurt her, he'd done nothing but hold her all night. There was an empty hole next to her. She felt as though someone had died.

Rising slow, her breath hitched as shooting pains from her side and arm got the best of her. Too much activity yesterday after sitting in a hospital bed for over a week.

Next to the bed, lay her pain pills and a glass of water along with a note.

Take these...don't be stubborn. Call me when you get up.
~Love you, Sam

Glaring at the note, she complied, then shuffled to the bathroom and stared at her ragged reflection. If she was gonna compete for Sam, she'd better try a little harder to look attractive.

Checking the time, she took a quick shower. Twenty-five minutes later, her hair was straight and shiny blonde, makeup on and dressed in her favorite black pants and a form fitting blue shirt. One she knew Sam loved.

Kirin stared at her jewelry box. Staring back was her shiny diamond engagement ring. She wasn't supposed to be engaged anymore, so she closed the lid and shook her head. Just a few months earlier she dreaded wearing it to work. Now it was all she wanted.

Will ambled down the hall toward the bathroom. The aroma Rosa's warm waffles and crispy bacon kickstarted one eye open and made him sniff the air like a dog. She was sure he was only half awake when she squeezed him, but when he held her tight for several seconds longer than usual, she knew he was glad to have her home. Afterward she bounded toward Little Jack's room to tickle him out of bed.

Kirin needed to rush to physical therapy after driving Will to school. Hospital HR had insisted she take the rest of the week off, so she planned to catch up and get her world back turning.

Downstairs she grabbed a cup from the cupboard. It was bare without all of Sam's cups. She pushed the sadness down, poured some coffee and sat at the bar.

"Morning," Kirin said into her coffee.

Rosa eyed her, "You look nice. Going somewhere today?"

"After therapy, I'm gonna drop by and see Maggie."

"Ah," Rosa said, busying her hands with buttering waffles.

"What?"

"It's just…you look nice for a trip to see your Aunt. Especially since Sam is out of town." Rosa lifted one eyebrow.

"He is?"

"You didn't know?" She stopped buttering.

"No," Kirin snapped, not so much at Rosa but at the idea that someone knew where her fiancé was, and she didn't.

"Did he say where he was going?"

Rosa thought for a second, "No…not really…to visit an old friend, maybe? He just said to watch you and make sure you didn't get into any trouble."

"Jerk," she said to herself, sipping the hot coffee.

Rosa walked toward her as Will and Little Jack bounded down the steps.

"Don't think for one minute that everything he's doing, isn't for you. Because it is."

Great, even Rosa knew more about the situation than she did. "You know if he'd talk to me and maybe include me, then I wouldn't worry he was doing something bad."

With her.

Will ran in and inhaled breakfast faster than any kid she'd ever seen. She stared at him like he had three heads. "What's the rush?"

"Gotta get there early, mom. We play paper football before the bell rings and I'm in the lead."

Her competitive little man.

She kissed Little Jack who shoved forkfuls of waffles in his mouth and then Rosa. Only since Saul had died in her backyard, and Kirin had the accident had Rosa become more open to adult hugs.

Will ran to the garage, threw his backpack in the back and honked the horn. Kirin leveled a look at him before climbing inside.

Kirin got her rear handed to her at Physical Therapy. Afterward, she needed a drink to take another dose of pain meds. The sadistic PT had made her contort her body into a pretzel and her arm throbbed in time with her heartbeat. She pulled into her favorite quickie mart on her way to Maggie's downtown shop.

Just as she was about to pull open the glass door, it opened for her. She glanced up and politely said, "Thank you," to the woman holding the door. It wasn't until she crossed the threshold, Kirin realized the woman looked familiar. She looked back and noticed the smug look on the woman's face.

Heading for the coffee station toward the back, she stopped in her tracks. Sam poured coffee into his mug. He turned and froze.

He was there…with *her*.

Jealousy sprinted through her body like electricity. If looks could kill, he'd be dead. She bit her cheek and shook her head, brushing past him. The first cup she pulled out of the holder, crumpled under the grip she had on it. Chucking it in the trash with gusto, she pulled a second cup down, a little gentler. Sam didn't move a muscle—as if he'd been seen by a T-Rex closing in on him.

The glass door shut with a thud and Kirin glanced back. The dark-haired home-wrecker strolled slowly to her black convertible carrying her drink. Bitch was laughing, too.

Kirin turned back and filled her coffee. She would not cry. Sam glanced at the door then scooted over behind her, grazing his stomach muscles across the top of her back. He leaned over and placed his coffee cup on the counter next to her.

Fury swept across her as he spoke.

"You smell amazing. You're wearing my favorite shirt… Hey, how was therapy?" he placed his hand on her waist while grabbing the sugar off the counter with his free hand.

She turned slow, like he'd slapped her in the face. Her mouth gaped. He must have a screw loose.

"Are you…tell me you're not serious right now? *Screw off,* Sam. You have no idea how hard this is to stand here and watch. Get away from me with your *girlfriend.*"

She turned, breaking his grasp and stomped to the island station where the good creamer was kept. She bit her cheek harder to keep the tears at bay. After using too much creamer, she fastened the lid at breakneck speed. She needed to get out of there and she didn't want to look at him again. She'd cried enough tears for the entire year, and she was not doing it again.

Her heart was hardening by the second.

Sam sighed loud, stopped next to her and added creamer to his coffee, silently. There was nothing he could say. Her jealous side reared its ugly head.

"Were you gonna tell me you were going out of town with *her*? You know what? Don't answer that. I don't care."

As she stomped around him toward the cashier, Sam grabbed her. Shielded from the view of the parking lot by a tall display of chips, he yanked the cup out of her hand and pulled her to him, hard. His mouth found hers and kissed her, deeply. Her mind fought him at first, pushing against his chest, but her body apparently had other plans.

One of his strong hands held her face while the other was wrapped tight around her waist, holding her body against his. Her arms changed trajectory from pushing on his chest to intertwining in his hair. The moans from their lips were quiet, but she felt his body harden against hers. Faintly, she heard the cashier clear his throat and realized what a spectacle they'd made.

Shaking and gasping for air, she broke contact first. She pushed off his chest, grabbed her coffee and ran for the cashier. She practically threw the money at the poor man and ran out the door.

Gianna's convertible was parked in the spot closest to the door. Her long, dark hair was pulled back in a low, stylish ponytail. Her face looked older and more worn than Kirin had imagined it would.

The wench was checking herself in her visor mirror and glanced up as Kirin trotted out, red faced, disheveled and perfectly kissed. Kirin smiled her best, "eat shit" smile and climbed into her car. As she backed out, Gianna's stare switched from Kirin to Sam. He looked even more messed up than she did, with his hair standing on end and Kirin's lipstick smeared all over his lips.

As she drove off, she glanced in the rear view mirror and saw him standing on the sidewalk with a satisfied smile, watching her taillights disappear.

Chapter Eleven

When her heart rate slowed, and she'd taken her pain medicine, she opened her window to clear her head. The cool autumn air did wonders. What the hell was that? It'd been a while since they'd made love—days before the accident—but whatever that was...was powerful.

Her lips were puffy. She touched them and felt the deep kiss. Yes... he loved her. She'd promised she'd remember. But that all flew out the window when she saw him with Gianna. This was too hard—knowing that snake knew about her and yet she monopolized his time trying to steal him away.

She shook the images out of her head and got back to the task at hand. She headed towards Maggie's store. Maybe she could weasel some information about Saul's extended family. She just needed a clue as to what kind of person she was up against. She needed to determine who the ringleader was, Scar or Todd, or if it was someone else she hadn't encountered yet. She had to discover the hierarchy to know how to get her friend back.

Kirin parked in the garage and walked down the steps toward Market Square zipping her jacket against the morning air as best she could with one arm. It was opening time and her Aunt Maggie should be flitting around inside *Galaxy 10*.

When she reached the door, the sign still read, "Closed." She checked her watch again then cupped her hands to look in the window. Lights were burning in her office, but the main store lights were off.

She yanked on the door, but it was locked. Then, she whipped out her key and tapped it three times on the glass. Nothing. Pulling out her phone, she dialed her aunt's number. On the third ring, her aunt answered in a whisper.

"Aunt Maggie?"

"Who is this?" she replied, tight and angry.

"Kirin, your niece."

"Oh, dear, I'm sorry. I've been spooked this morning. What can I do for you dear?"

"I'm standing outside the shop, but your door is locked."

Kirin watched as her Aunt's head popped out from inside her office. She waved and waddled toward the door. Her flowered skirt and sweater swayed back and forth, as she came closer to the door. Maggie unlocked it, ushered Kirin inside then locked it back, turning around and hugging Kirin, tight.

"Dear… I'm so sorry I didn't visit you in the hospital. Then, I didn't get a chance to speak to you much at your party. I should've come up there, but my anxiety got me. I'm sorry."

"Oh, don't worry about that. What's got you so spooked this morning?" Kirin placed a hand on her aunt's shoulder.

Maggie hesitated, her eyes darting around. A tell-tale sign that Kirin was about to get only half the truth.

"Oh nothing, just crazy downtown bums walking in and looking around like they want to rob me. I'll open the doors now that you are here. We can sit up front and chat for a bit, okay?"

Maggie flitted past and switched on the lights, plugging in a few Halloween displays and unlocking the door before returning. They sat on stools and leaned over the glass case up front and watched people walk by.

Kirin took a breath and got to the point. "Maggie, I need some information from you."

Maggie eyed Kirin over the top of her glasses.

"Sam said no. He's already warned me that you'd be here asking questions. He made me promise I wouldn't tell you anything about Saul's wretched family."

Kirin's jaw tightened. She sat up straight on her stool shaking her head.

"Did he also tell you that he's moved out, broken up with me and was seeing another woman behind my back while I was in the hospital?"

Maggie cocked her head to the side, "No...wait, that doesn't make any sense, why would he do that? Are you serious?"

She lifted her ringless left hand. Maggie's eyes grew wide.

For all purposes, this was the story they were supposed to live by, so why not tell Maggie? The whole family would know by Sunday when he wouldn't show up to their normal family Sunday dinner, so why not use this information to her benefit?

"So, whatever he told you, doesn't count. He's gone."

Maggie scratched her head and looked around her shop for some divine inspiration. She let out a defeating breath and watched Kirin through dark rimmed glasses.

"What do you want to know?"

Kirin thought for a moment. "When Saul died, who would've been next in line to take over?"

Maggie walked over to the cash register and grabbed her drink, walking back, her eyes narrowed, deep in thought. A sadness crossed her face. She still felt responsible for Saul's death.

"Well, let's see... there was Nicky...Nicola is his full name. He was Saul's younger brother. He was a little...odd. Super shy around me. He never spoke but watched Saul and I all the time. His parents used to send him with us on dates as our chaperone. I'd think he'd be in line to be the head unless Saul had a son."

"He did...Todd. He's engaged to my friend Stacy. Or I think they're married now, I'm not sure. She hasn't spoken to me since the night..." Kirin trailed off.

Maggie stared at her hands.

"What I need to know is who's pulling the strings."

Kirin told her about feeling like Stacy was forced to stay away, about the flowers in the hospital, and the phone call leading to catching Sam in the parking lot. She left out the part about Stacy texting her, just in case Sam called Maggie, but told her about the threatening phone calls she and Sam were getting.

Maggie looked horrified.

"Kirin… I think I know who's running the show. But…" Maggie hesitated, staring off into the distance. "I'm not completely sure."

"Who?"

"Sam mentioned that he heard Nicky oversaw the drug side now, but he wasn't the leader; however, with the hospital bombing, I can't help but think that's wrong. He has the *demeanor* for cruel punishment and although I've never met Saul's son, I'd say Nicky would be the one to worry about. But, Saul's son and Nicky aren't the only heirs."

"Really? Who else?

"A woman…although Saul's dad would roll over in his grave, Sam mentioned a woman."

Kirin rolled her eyes, "Yep. Same one he kissed at the hospital, I'm sure."

Maggie shot Kirin a look of pity and touched her hand. The lump in her throat burned. Then Maggie glanced down at her skirt and straightened it out. "Okay, I lied to you earlier. I actually…Well, I saw a man this morning in front of my shop, from the past.

"I had the closed sign out, but the door was unlocked. All the lights were off, but I was standing right here in the shadow fixing the display. This man walked by twice, slow, which always makes me take notice, so I won't get robbed again. On the third pass he stopped and cupped his hands on the window and looked inside."

Maggie took a deep breath. "It was Nicky."

"Are you sure it was him? You haven't seen him in what…forty years?"

"True… and it's possible I'm wrong. But he looked in, then slid his hand around the doorknob at the exact second I remembered it wasn't locked. I panicked. He turned the door handle but stopped. Then he stepped back and glanced up at my apartment." She shuddered and exhaled, clearly rattled.

"It was like he was working out a puzzle. Then he turned to the right and the sun caught his scar. I knew it was him. He sprinted away right before you called."

Scar. Chills ran up Kirin's arms. Scar's name was Nicky. Scar suited him better. So, if Nicky was in charge, he was solely responsible for the cafeteria bombing and Laura's coma. Then it hit her.

"If he left right before I called... then he saw me walk in here. It'd confirm his hunch that this was your shop." Kirin ran a trembling hand through her hair.

"I'm so sorry...I've led him right to your door."

"Oh, honey, I think he knew where I was before he ever saw you here," she added sadly. "I might just have to take a good long vacation for a bit and get my assistant manager to run the place for a while. They couldn't mistake her for me, she's young and skinny with green hair, and pierced *everywhere*. She won't be in any danger," Maggie smiled wearily.

"I'm so sorry," Kirin repeated. "Where will you go?"

Maggie patted her on the shoulder. "Dear, the less you know the better. Don't worry about me, your dad made sure I had several escape plans already thought out a long time ago. Most of which involve a nice vacation destination. I will worry about you though.

"I'm sure Nicky believes Saul's death was not only my fault but yours and Sam's. You two need to work this out and come together as a team instead of against each other. And Kirin, don't underestimate Nicky."

Kirin picked up her phone and dialed Sam. Shit, she forgot—he was still with *her*. He answered on the first ring.

"Hello?" his voice was clipped.

"Look, I know you can't talk on your *date*, but I need security placed on Maggie. Can you help me, or should I call Steve?"

"I can do it," he said indignantly.

"Thank you."

"Thank *you* for this morning," she heard a faint smile on his lips. Bet that perplexed the wench. "We're still on for tomorrow night, right?" he asked formally as if he was talking to a business associate.

"Uh...no. I've got plans."

"Not anymore you don't."

"You're an infuriating man."

"Seven? Yeah, seven sounds great," he said, ignoring her.

"I won't be home," she lied.

"Sure, I'll meet you there," he said, then the phone line went dead.

Kirin stared at her cell, then looked up to see Maggie smiling.

"Well, it's good you two are speaking. Now you run along back home but watch your back. I'll lock the door back and pack up. Knowing Sam, he'll have someone here in a few minutes."

She'd just found her father's sister, not even six months earlier, and she was losing her again. Kirin shook her head no, frozen. She didn't want to say goodbye.

Maggie stepped toward her, "Honey, it'll all be fine. I'll send you a postcard when I get settled. Knowing that impatient crew, it won't take them long to give up on me and when it's all over, I'll come back. I promise." Maggie kissed her cheek and handed over her hoodie. Kirin gave her one more, quick squeeze.

"I'll be waiting for that post card," she said, memorizing Maggie's features before she turned around. Maggie unlocked the door and Kirin walked out into the October cold.

~*~

Heading toward her car, she was on high alert. Scar, or Nicky as Maggie called him, was in the vicinity only a few minutes before. Any sudden movement and she'd use the mace on her keychain, which was out and wrapped around her hand. She needed a gun. Sam wore one, why couldn't she?

Rounding a concrete pole, she spotted a woman leaning up against the back of her SUV. She slowed, squinting so the woman's face came into focus. The woman's arms were crossed in a pissed-off stance.

Kirin strode toward her, shoulders back, but mace out and her head on a swivel. This woman could very well be bait. Her heart thudded. When she got close, the woman smiled, but her eyes were misty as if she'd been crying.

Kirin came to a halt several feet away.

"What? What do you want?"

If Stacy was startled by her tone, she didn't flinch. "We need to talk." She sounded tired.

"Is this a set-up? Is some thug gonna jump out and hurt me?"

Stacy uncrossed her arms and stood tall, "Kirin, why would you say that? I'd never do that. Really? That's what you think of me?"

"I don't know what to think. Laura is still in a coma because of you."

Stacy threw her arms in the air, "I *told you* over text—that wasn't me! Or Todd. It was…someone else. Todd doesn't have anything to do with the barbaric side of the business. He runs the money part. Admittedly, he's not your biggest fan or Sam's, but he swore he didn't order the hit on you."

Kirin stepped towards her.

"And you believe him? Stace, wake up. He took Saul's place. Saul had my mother killed and my father enslaved in The Club his entire life. He was forced to abandon me, or else Saul would've had me killed as a child. Don't you see? I didn't kill Saul. His grief did. He learned, the love of his life was alive and didn't want him, and he took his own life. It wasn't me."

Stacy's eyebrows pinched together. "I didn't know he ordered your mom's death or took your dad from you," Stacy stared down at the pavement. "I'm sorry. I was only told he died…and it was your fault. Todd was devastated. He cried for weeks."

Stacy shifted from foot to foot. "I miss you," she admitted, "and I miss Laura. My world is so different now. If I could go back to before Todd's father died, I'd do it in a heartbeat."

"I wouldn't. That was a terrifying time for me. Saul hunted me down and put a gun to my head. I'm just lucky he didn't pull the trigger."

"Why didn't you tell us? I could've helped. Steve could've helped." Stacy took a cautious step toward Kirin.

"I didn't know Saul was Todd's father until your dinner party. And Steve did help. He brought the FBI to my house and saved us." Kirin shoved cold hands into her pockets. She shook more from the conversation than the chill in the air. She was afraid to ask but had to know. "Why did you act so odd in the cafeteria? You held my hand under the table, and pushed me?"

"A show. I wanted to give Todd's uncle a show. I had strict orders, in front of his uncle, not to speak with you if I happened to see you out."

"Stacy, why would you take *orders* from Todd to do anything?"

Stacy stared at her shoes. "Our relationship has gone through some changes." She locked eyes with Kirin. "I belong to him…with him. He still treats me like a queen in private, but I have boundaries now. Places I can go and people I can see. And others… I can't."

Kirin's eyes narrowed. Her friend was a slave in Todd's world. She had to get her out, but how? She needed to know what they held over her head to convince her to live like this, but first, they needed to be able to trust each other.

"So you can't be seen with me, but we can still be friends?" Kirin's voice was a hoarse whisper thanks to the lump in her throat.

Stacy's eyes perked up, "Yes! Would you consider that kind of a friendship? A temporary arrangement until I can convince Todd to go back to the way things were. He's a good man, Kirin, really, he's just fallen into this odd culture right now, but I know I can bring him back out."

Even if this was a trap, she couldn't leave Stacy in this situation. She had to get her out.

Kirin smiled, "I'll take your friendship however I can get it."

Stacy ran to her friend, lifted her off the ground and hugged her, crying and laughing at the same time. When she placed her back on the ground, she glanced at her watch, ran back to a bright red sports car, and peeled out, waving.

Kirin stared after the taillights.

She'd make sure Stacy was out right before she crushed these people.

Chapter Twelve

Driving home, Kirin thought of Sam. Where was he going with the wench today? Gianna had looked so smug, as if she'd already won. She needed to know more about her foe to be able to win. So far, all she had was the woman was an attorney in Cleveland. She didn't know her last name or even where she fit in with Saul's clan, but she knew what she was. A prostitute, just like Sam. Only, from the way he spoke, she was dug in deeper than he'd been.

At the top of her to-do list was to see how many Gianna's she could find practicing Law in Cleveland.

She pulled in to find Little Jack asleep and Rosa napping on the couch in front of the TV, while pretending to watch her "stories."

Kirin crept upstairs, tossed her things on her bed, and fired up her computer. Checking her watch, she had an hour before she had to grab Will from school.

Googling the name "Gianna," "Law," and "Cleveland," the search engine found three possibilities. The Rhodes and Lambert Law firm, Testerman Law, and Calamia and Associates. Calamia was Saul's last name. That was easy.

She clicked on the Calamia Law firm. Pictures of seven attorneys came up along with a professional, model-like picture of the wench. Great. She was the owner of the firm specializing in labor law, divorce and workers compensation law. Snatching up the number, she dialed. Since she was traveling with Sam, most likely she wasn't there.

The receptionist answered, "Calamia and Associates, Leah speaking."

"Hi Leah, Is Miss Gianna Calamia in today?"

"No, Ma'am. Most of our attorneys are gone this afternoon to prepare for the benefit."

"Benefit?" she asked.

"Yes, Ma'am. The annual benefit that Attorney Calamia sponsors to help girls affected by human trafficking. If you'd like to donate, you can watch the benefit online tonight or if you're local in Cleveland, it will be broadcast on PBS at 7pm."

"Great, thank you." Kirin would bet her last dollar that Sam's suit was gone out of the cabin. They were headed to Cleveland so he could be arm candy for the wench. Great. She picked up a piece of mail, crammed it into a ball and threw it as hard as she could. She felt like a jealous girl in middle school. She glanced up at the ceiling. What would a punching bag look like hanging in the middle of her bedroom?

If this double life crap lasted much longer, she may need to invest in one.

Her phone buzzed with a new text:

"You said you'd remember…looking forward to tomorrow night. –S"

If she could have thrown her phone without breaking it, she would've. She couldn't even scream with two family members asleep downstairs.

She wrote back. *"I told you, I won't be home. Have fun at the benefit."*

Three dots popped up, meaning he was writing back, but then disappeared. Served him right. Then again, she could try to see this with an objective eye. See it for what it was. He was keeping her alive. She wanted to punch him though, all the same.

An hour later, with a sleepy-eyed Little Jack in her car, Kirin picked Will up from school. He began talking as soon as the door slammed. It was so interesting to see the world through his eyes. The dynamic of his friends and their adult like conversations amazed her.

"Mom, can you sign me up for Karate? Robert takes it and I've been dying to start."

"Sure buddy," she said absentmindedly.

"That way if the bad people ever come back, I can defend us."

Kirin could only stare ahead. He knew... He was perceptive enough to know about the danger last time and to know it might come again.

"Hey, Will," she began, "Did you ever hear Sam talking on the phone to anyone while I was in the hospital?" Will was crouched over in his seat feverishly doing his math homework, only half listening.

"A few." He said not offering any information. "Mom, what's seven times eight?"

"Fifty-six." She answered, then asked a different question, "Did you ever hear Sam talking to a woman?"

"No..." She let out a breath. Good.

"But I did," he added.

Kirin almost stopped the car in the middle of the road. "When did you talk to a *woman*?"

Will was concentrating on his homework and had to be asked twice.

"Will?"

"What?" he asked innocently.

She repeated the question, "Son, when did you speak to a woman on the phone?"

"Um...when you were in the hospital, I think. Sam was in the backyard fixing the grill and the home phone rang. A woman asked for you. I told her you weren't home. She asked what hospital you were in because she wanted to send you flowers, I told her 'St. Mary's'."

The harlot called her house. And weaseled information from her child. The nerve. She could've spit fire.

They drove home, finished homework, and ate dinner. As she cleaned the dishes, Will played a few games on the PS4 with Little Jack. But they argued and had to be separated. She flicked on the cable to see if they had the same programing as Cleveland, but theirs was a symphony at seven, so she got the boys settled and went upstairs to see if she could stream it through her laptop.

Seven o'clock on the dot, the camera closed in to show a smiling host dressed in a black tuxedo. Directly behind him was a three-tiered stage with rows of tables covered with satin tablecloths and telephones positioned every few feet. Smiling attendants waited for the phones to ring. The host spoke about how to donate and their monetary goals, as a toll-free number flashed at the bottom of the screen.

He went on to describe the destitute conditions Hispanic women were forced into when they tried to come to the U.S. to start a new life—only to be sold into slavery. He whispered in animated fashion as if he were introducing tigers to the world. More funding was needed to house and educate these young girls and to save those still missing. All the while the producers showed pictures of young dark-skinned girls with large haunted eyes.

Panning out, the shot included men and women on the dance floor moving gracefully in sparkling beaded gowns and tuxedos. Kirin squinted, trying to spot Sam. Then the host announced he'd be introducing the partners and interviewing Miss Gianna Calamia herself, the champion of the fundraiser and owner of the law firm. She plugged in headphones, so she could hear Gianna's voice and her answers. Time to size this woman up.

After all the other attorney's and their wives had been introduced, her breath hitched as the dark headed hustler, dripping in diamonds and Kirin's Sam walked toward the host.

A painted-on, sparkling, royal blue gown swung as she walked. The slit came dangerously close to letting the world see everything she had. Long, black scoops of hair had been pinned up, intertwined to look both regal and casual. The diamond necklace and earring set looked like they'd make Harry Winston drool. Once she'd had her fill of Gianna, Kirin's eyes caught Sam. He wore a form fitting black tuxedo with a matching blue tie and looked every bit the man of her dreams.

A stab of pain hit her chest. She'd never seen him in a tux before. She'd hoped to see him in one at their wedding, which seemed to be slipping farther and farther away. The more she stared, she realized how uncomfortable he looked as she clung to him like a cheap suit.

The host spoke of Gianna's contributions and passion to help the Hispanic community. He asked her why supporting these young girls was so important.

"People close to my heart have been through this horror. No woman should be sold against her will. They deserve a good life and to get the care and help they need. This atrocity needed a champion, a spotlight if you will, to highlight it and give it the same attention some of the other causes in our country receive."

The host looked down at his card then over at Sam. "Miss Calamia, would you like to introduce your date?"

Gianna held tight to Sam's arm and cooed. "This is Sam Neal, my boyfriend and soon to be much more."

"Well congratulations!" The host gushed. Sam looked like he was about to throw up.

Kirin's fists balled. Gianna was putting him through hell on purpose, assuming he was hers. Her smile indicated she loved watching him squirm. Well, two could play at that game.

~*~

When the phones rang, and the donations began rolling in, most were in memory of someone who had passed, or in thanksgiving for a young daughter or niece who lived a free life.

Sam had gradually bowed out of the limelight and stood off to the side near the phones while Gianna and the host read the tributes coming in with the donations.

"$50.00 in honor of Tanner and Catie Cardwell and their two kids," Gianna read.

"$25.00 in memoriam for Leah's great Aunt Brooke," The host read.

Then a phone attendant ran down and handed Gianna a note. Kirin smiled and propped her feet up on her desk and watched.

"$250.00! Whoa!" She smiled big for the camera. "Now that's the kind of donations we need! Okay, let's see…$250.00 in honor of Sam Neal and the deep passionate kiss in the quickie mart this morning and to the dark-headed woman who held the door."

Gianna's face fell as she glared at the camera. Conveniently, Sam moved from his spot just inside camera range, and like magic, her phone rang.

"Hello." She answered cheerfully, thinking about popping open a leftover bottle of wine to celebrate the small victory.

"What the hell are you doing?" Sam asked, sounding more amused than angry.

"What? Human Trafficking is a serious crime, Sam."

Sam howled. "You're gonna get us both killed, you know that?"

"Oh, no…" Kirin hadn't thought about the repercussions for Sam when she'd thrown away $250 to prove a point. "…will she take this out on you?"

"Probably on both of us, but I really don't care," he said, wearily. "I'm just ready to get this over with and come home. I've got everything I needed to get on this trip. Kirin?"

"Yeah?"

"Do us both a favor—turn it off. Shit… gotta go."

The phone line went dead. The camera had panned away from the host and into the dancing crowd as a beautiful young woman stood on the stage in front of the phones and sang a haunting slow song. Gianna sauntered across the dance floor in her blue sparkling dress holding hands with Sam. She should've turned it off. She knew what Giana would do. With her hand on the mouse hovering over the x, she couldn't bring herself to close the program.

They began dancing as the camera panned from couple to couple and then back to the singer a few times. As soon as the camera panned over to Sam and Gianna she laid her head on his shoulder and snuggled in close. He leaned down and planted a kiss on her forehead, and she grinned widely for the camera.

Kirin turned it off, cursing herself for not turning it off when he asked her to.

That would be a difficult image to erase out of her memory.

Chapter Thirteen

The nerve. She'd give it to her though, Kirin had a vindictive streak. Kind of reminded her of herself. But didn't that *southern hick* know she was out of her depth? Gianna had never lost a case. And she had never intended to lose Sam from the start. Her record was spotless—and in this arena, it'd be no different.

Stupid woman. Sam didn't seem to notice though. Especially when Gianna was dolled up in her tight dress and heels.

Kirin couldn't possibly think she could compete. Surely she wasn't that naïve. She was a short, plain nurse in a small town with a plain kids and a plain face. No match for Gianna's power, status, and wealth.

But Sam. Sam was baiting Gianna, and she knew it. But that had always been their relationship. If she could just convince him to take it one *tiny* step further, she'd have him all to herself. The time would come. She was sure of it.

But there were bigger fish to fry.

Almost time to right all the wrongs.

Chapter Fourteen

Tuesday morning, Kirin woke with a jolt. She'd *felt* Sam sleeping next to her, she knew it. She'd even stayed to her side of the bed like he was there. But his side was empty. Had to be a dream, but she'd been so warm, wrapped around him with his arms holding her.

Blinking sleep out of her eyes, her wine bottle and glass were gone. Her laptop was closed, but she didn't remember closing it. It was like a clean-up ghost had been there and whisked things away while she slept. She'd been hot from the wine when she went to bed, but now covers lay on top of her.

No sign of Sam though. Part of her wished he'd left the benefit, drove all night, and slept next to her in the early morning hours. But she wasn't that lucky.

Kirin got up, dressed and ready in record time. Heading downstairs, Rosa made crockpot oatmeal and coffee gurgled while Will gathered his backpack. Her cell slept on the wireless charger but flashed with messages.

The first was from Stacy's new number. She'd told Kirin she'd snuck out and bought a new cell which nobody in Todd's fortress could trace. The message had come in at midnight. Kirin's face scrunched as she listened to her message. She sounded depressed:

"Hey, K, it's me. Can we meet this week? I need to talk. Text me."

The second message was from Chuck, one of the crusty, almost retired TWRA guys who worked with Sam. It had come in ten minutes earlier. He sounded like he was sitting inside a jet engine but recognized it as the roar of his truck.

"Kirin, this is Chuck over at TWRA. Listen, I hate to call you so early, but Sam was supposed to meet me at six to check our traps up on Sharps Ridge. He hasn't shown up yet. I tried his cell but didn't get an answer. I think he's overslept. Could you have him call me? I'm running to grab a coffee but should be in the truck. Thanks."

It was ten after seven. He'd probably overslept from driving back so late from Cleveland, but it wasn't like him to not hear his cell. Alarms went off in the back of her mind. She picked up the house phone and dialed his cell. No answer. Then, she dialed the cabin number. On the third ring it sounded like he dropped the phone and then picked it back up...

The female voice she recognized all too well, cooed, "Hello? Hello?"

Kirin slammed down the phone. Rosa stopped moving and stared. Kirin shook from head to toe, fists balled. When she exhaled and stomped into the pantry, Rosa followed.

"Did he answer?" Rosa whispered, wide-eyed.

"No, *she* did." She hated even saying the words. Tears threatened to fall, and she bit the inside of her cheek, staring anywhere but at Rosa. Something in her belly twisted. Her mind snapped. The wench had won.

Rosa hung her head. "I'm so sorry. I don't know what to say."

"I'm sorry too. I can't play second fiddle anymore." Kirin sucked in a ragged breath. "I give up. She can have him."

"Now, wait a minute. You're jumping to conclusions. What if he didn't stay there? And what if he's just running late this morning? Maybe she slept at the cabin and he didn't sleep? You know sometimes he can't sleep. Or..." Rosa was grasping at any shred of hope she could give Kirin. But it was too late. Kirin shook her head no, but Rosa continued, "He could've slept in his car. He could have been sleeping here for all we know, then got up late and hasn't turned the ringer back on for his cell."

Yes, if all the stars aligned in perfect harmony, the love of her life didn't just sleep with the prostitute. But in her chaotic imperfect life, had that ever happened?

Kirin trudged out of the pantry to check the history on the alarm system. It was set by her at 11:00 and then disarmed by Rosa at 6:30 this morning. He didn't stay there.

Will stood in the kitchen watching them whisper at the front door near the alarm, looking confused. His eyes were still puffy from sleep.

"What are you guys doing?"

Kirin startled, then said, "Nothing son, just talking about our system."

Rosa ushered him back to the bar to start his breakfast while she walked back into the pantry. Kirin stared at the canned foods while it hit her. Gianna's voice still echoed in her head. She won. Kirin refused to cry. *Acceptance, perseverance and move on.*

Walking back into the kitchen, she opened the cupboard for a cup. One of Sam's old cups rested inside. Must have been missed when he took his things. She pulled it down and wrapped both hands around it like it was her lifeline. She'd use this one today to help her say goodbye.

No matter his good intentions to keep her safe, she couldn't be with a man who slept with other women.

She drove Will to school, then went to physical therapy numbly. The therapist pushed her and her arm way past the comfort zone. She didn't care. She wrote Stacy back and asked where they could meet.

"Rogers Bar?" Stacy suggested.

Rogers was a small, seedy, neighborhood bar not far from her house. Mainly regulars frequented the place since it was behind a strip mall and not that many people knew about it. Sam would never think to look there.

"Sounds like a perfectly terrible idea. What time?"

"Six," she wrote, adding a smiley face.

"Meet you there."

Kirin's phone buzzed with a short text from Aunt Kathy. The woman loathed texting and was horrible at it. She thought everything was supposed to be an acronym like "lol." Her cryptic texts were like a riddle you had to solve. It was as if she thought she was charged by the word.

"K – CM-INTTTY"

Kirin laughed... only her Aunt Kathy could put a whole sentence in nine letters. She dialed her number.

"Hello?"

"Why can't you text like a normal person?" Kirin chided her, giggling.

"Oh, Kirin you can get that one, it's easy."

"I get the CM for Call me. After that, I'm lost."

"It was, "*I Need to Talk To You.*"

"Why can't you just type that?"

"Because, what fun would that be and...it worked. You called me."

"By default, because I couldn't understand your cryptic text!"

Her Aunt Kathy laughed. It always took her back to her mom's laugh when she did.

She continued, "Honey, Dean's at work but he wanted me to call you and see if we could get the boys after school and keep them here tonight. He said he, Will and Little Jack are all working on Halloween costumes and since Dean's gotta work this weekend, he wondered if we could keep them, so they can finish. I know it's a school night, so we'll take Will to school tomorrow and I'll keep Little Jack until you wake up. Maybe give Rosa a day to herself, too?"

Selfishly, she hated the idea of sleeping in her big house alone, but this way Rosa could have a day off, the boys could have a mid-week treat and she could spend more time with Stacy.

"They'd love that! Thank you." Then it dawned on her.

"Aunt Kathy, did Sam put Uncle Dean up to this?"

She hesitated, which was a bad sign. "Um, I don't know, but Sam did call Dean last night. Sam had him absolutely howling about something."

Glad they got a kick out of her donation. Too bad it'd backfired on her.

"Aunt Kathy, I don't…I don't think Sam and I are gonna make it." Kirin's voice cracked at the end, even though she'd tried hard to keep emotion out of it.

Her Aunt Kathy stuttered, "Well…honey, love makes us do some idiotic things. Sam is a good man and he loves you, that I know for sure. Whatever he's doing, I'm positive he thinks it's the right thing to keep you safe."

Her tears were hot and stinging. "I just don't know if I can forgive him…" She whispered into the phone and felt like she was eight again, crying to her stand-in mama.

Kathy was silent for a moment. "Wanna come over? We can have a cup of coffee and talk?"

"I'll be right there."

Two cups of coffee and an hour later, she left Kathy and Dean's feeling like her brain was tired, but slightly better about her situation. Her aunt had become one of those "cup all the way full" kind of people and you couldn't help but feel more positive about your circumstances after spending an hour with her. She climbed back into her car and found three missed calls and two texts from Sam.

The text's read:

"I can't wait to see you tonight."

And

"How did therapy go?"

Kirin couldn't help but to write back.

"Where did you sleep last night, Sam?"

The reply came back immediately, *"What little sleep I got, was in bed."*

She'd bet. Her face felt red and hot. She tossed her phone into the seat next to her after turning the ringer off.

When she got home, Rosa left early, and Kirin busied herself by playing games with Little Jack. When he went down for his nap, she rummaged her closet looking for something spectacular to wear. Even though it was just Roger's Bar, Stacy would be dressed impeccably, and she wanted just one person to notice her. Maybe she'd feel pretty again.

Her favorite green top. It fit fabulously and hugged her curves. It was scoop necked, three quarter sleeved, and loose and flirty around the hem. It would look perfect with black leggings and her worn-in brown cowboy boots. She was looking forward to seeing her old friend. They'd texted a few times since Stacy had bought her new phone and her friend was desperate to tell her something.

Kirin's house phone rang, and she darted downstairs to grab it before it woke Little Jack. He'd be a bear at Kathy and Dean's if he woke early.

Out of breath, she answered, "Hello?"

"I think we need to talk, don't you?" Gianna's silky voice hummed in her ear.

"About what, exactly?" Kirin snapped, perturbed. *Doesn't this woman have a job?*

"About the man we seem to be sharing."

"We aren't sharing him. You're using him as arm candy. He's mine. And don't you have better things to do? Your job must be very flexible—seems like you never work."

"I own the company, dear. I work when I want." She said snobbishly.

"Convenient for you. Were you really going to visit me in the hospital? What kind of a home-wrecker are you?" Kirin asked, raising her voice.

"One that always gets what she wants. By *any* means necessary. So I'm gonna cut you a deal …one that I know you won't be able to turn down. I'm sure you love Sam, and I can tell he has *feelings* for you, too. The Club, well…they want his head for double crossing Saul. Of course, they want yours too, but I can guarantee Sam's safety. Nobody would touch him, ever. But you'd have to leave him. And you couldn't tell him why."

Kirin sat slow on a stool at the bar. Gianna was right. Kirin loved him, and she couldn't imagine life without him. Her nightmares had been all about Sam dying. Which meant her subconscious worried constantly about his safety. Somewhere in the back of her mind, she knew The Club would come after them, but the idea of Sam dying and leaving her here to grieve was more than she could stand. She'd already been there with her mama, Jack, and her father. She couldn't lose Sam too.

There had to be a way around this. The line went silent as she mulled it over. But what about her boys? How would they survive without her and Sam? And what if they came after her Aunt Kathy and Uncle Dean? They would. She knew they would. She'd have to save them all, even if she herself didn't survive. How much did Gianna want Sam?

"Counteroffer. Me and my family, *all* my family— guarantee our safety too. No retaliation on any of us, no matter what."

You could hear the smile erupting in her voice, "Done. So that's a yes?"

"Give me twenty-four hours to think about it."

"Nope. Midnight. The number on your caller ID is my cell, write it down and call me *before* midnight. One last thing... you'd better be a damn good actress and break his heart in two. He has to believe that you *really* mean it, I don't want him pining for you as I pick up the pieces."

Kirin laid the receiver down without another word. She sat all alone in her kitchen with her head in her hands and wept.

Chapter Fifteen

By four-thirty, the boys were gone, the house was locked up and she was in the shower. Her dilemma had run through her mind all day, sidetracking her every move, causing her to spill her coffee, trip over the rug and burn the cheesy bread she'd made Little Jack for a snack after his nap.

At the end of it all, she knew. She'd protect him. They wouldn't have to worry any more about his safety. *They*—there'd be no more 'they,' only she and her boys. The power and confidence in Gianna's voice convinced her that the woman would stand by her promise.

Sam would be married to Gianna—to be her arm candy. But he'd be alive. If she took the deal, she wouldn't have to worry about the boys, her Aunt and Uncle, Rosa, or Maggie. Maggie could come back with no threat of retribution.

Kirin dried and straightened her hair, applied makeup, and pulled on leggings, her green top and boots. She checked her watch—five-thirty. She had a good twenty-minute drive in traffic to the bar. Grabbing her purse, she eyed Gianna's number laying on the counter, crumpled it and threw it into her purse before climbing in her car.

She'd ignored another two calls from Sam. A pinch in her gut warned her she was missing out on a last chance with him. How was she going to break it off clean, without showing her true feelings? She couldn't use the excuse that he'd slept with Gianna. He'd just deny it and she'd never know the truth. She had to think of something worse. Or was there another way to protect them all without losing him. Her mind pinged back and forth before focusing on grabbing a drink with her oldest friend. They'd figure out what to do together.

When Kirin pulled into the parking lot, it was almost empty. How many people frequent a neighborhood bar on a Tuesday? She felt foolish for dressing up. Stacy's red convertible was parked in the furthest spot from the road. She was hiding. Right next to it was a blacked-out sedan. Kirin parked hers next to the black one, shut off the car and trotted across the lot and into the bar.

Walking inside, her eyes struggled to adjust. One tall man sat with his back to her at the bar, wearing a suit. He didn't turn around when she entered. Roger's was small with just a half dozen tables sandwiched between the bar and the booths that hugged the wall all around the outside perimeter. She spotted Stacy sitting in a far booth, wearing Dolce & Gabbana sunglasses. Her Hermes black vintage bag wrapped around her too-thin frame and two empty shot glasses in front of her.

Stacy turned, her face exploded in a familiar toothy grin. Kirin's grin mimicked hers.

"You look amazing." Stacy gushed, slurring her words. The old Stacy was back.

"You look like a Bond girl waiting for her prey," Kirin hugged her friend then flopped and scooted into the other side of the booth, laughing.

Stacy removed the expensive sunglasses.

A black and purple circle hung perfectly around her right eye.

"What the hell?" Kirin asked, mouth gaping. "Did Todd do this to you?" It came out angrier than she meant.

"No…Yes….aw hell, I don't know how to explain. I had a perfectly good made-up story to tell you, but now my resolve is all screwed up after two of these babies." She pointed to the almost empty fireball shots.

"Son of a bitch," Kirin swore too loud. "You're coming back with me. And never going back to that prison, do you hear?" She noticed the man at the bar straightened.

An older woman, with a wrinkled face that told the world she didn't take anybody's crap, stomped up in perfect time. She stared from one woman to the other as if to say, "*Is there a problem*?" Both women sat back in unspoken tandem and grabbed the menus as if they were friends coming in for a beer after a hard day. Kirin ordered first.

"Can I get a bottle of Bud Light and chips and salsa to start?"

"Sure." The woman's tone was clipped. Then to Stacy "Another fireball?"

Stacy had snuck her sunglasses back on and stared at the menu. "Uh, no, can I get a beer like hers and chicken strips, please?" Stacy asked, her air of formality back.

The woman turned on her heel without another word. Stacy removed the sunglasses, Kirin couldn't take her eyes off the blue and purple hues coming from underneath her skin. Then it dawned on her.

"Did that happen because of me?" Kirin's hand flew to her open mouth, horrified. Although she could tell Stacy was planning to lie, her face revealed the truth.

"I didn't realize they had GPS tracking on all the fleet cars." She said nonchalantly. Todd's uncle spotted you at Market Square and then I showed up…they just put two and two together. Of course, I tried to lie my way out of it, but I'd *embarrassed* Todd in front of his uncle. He had to make a statement to show his strength or be considered weak…" her voice trailed off.

She was beaten because of Kirin. They were monsters.

"Yeah, beating a woman to show *strength*—I could break him like a twig." Kirin said through gritted teeth and stared at her own trembling hands.

Stacy exhaled and pointed to her eye, "this is actually tame compared…"

Their beers and chips were delivered, with a thud. It appeared that the bar lady wasn't thrilled with her choice of employment.

Kirin took a long draw of the beer. She couldn't skate around it any longer.

"Stacy, explain…Why do you stay there? I don't understand. He treats you like a slave and hits you. This isn't you. You've forgotten the bad ass you were just a few months ago." Kirin grabbed Stacy's hands. "She's in there telling you to walk away and kick the shit out of someone on your way out. But you're not listening to her, why?"

Stacy took a long breath and stared at their intertwined hands. The struggle on her face told Kirin she was waffling as to what to say.

"Stace, look at me." Her friend looked up. "It's me. I was wrong not to tell you and Laura about the trouble I was in back in the spring. About Saul and the book and my parents…I was afraid to burden you both with it. Please, don't make that same mistake…tell me." Kirin squeezed her hands.

Stacy exhaled, "It's like they've brainwashed Todd. He wasn't like this until his father died. The real him is in there somewhere. And they all know I want out. They've made it clear…if I leave, they'll hunt me down and kill me *slow*, but before I die, they'll get Steve, my parents… and *you* to die in front of me…for revenge." Stacy's voice trembled at the end. She picked up her beer, took a swig, then continued, "They have connections everywhere and the resources to do anything they want. There's only one way out," Stacy stared at the food, not looking at Kirin.

Rage ran through Kirin. The Club had been intimidating her family and friends since before she was born. Stacy was talking suicide. Her friend was contemplating taking her own life rather than try and stop what she felt was unstoppable.

It was time to end this.

"Shut up. You hear me? That's not an option. There are other ways out. And your brother has built a fortress around your parents. Nothing will get past him or the ten FBI agents he surrounds himself with…nobody is getting them or you."

"What about you?" she asked, after taking another long sip of beer. "Who'd protect you?

Kirin sipped to give her time to think. With Sam gone…nobody would protect her. She was completely on her own. She'd have to rely on her own instincts to survive. In her gut, she believed Gianna would stick to her word about protecting her family and friends, but something in her voice told Kirin that protection didn't include her.

If Stacy thought Kirin was alone, she'd never leave Todd. Kirin did what any best friend would do, she lied.

"I'll be fine. I've got Sam."

Stacy shot her a look as if to ask, "You sure?" She wondered what Stacy had heard about Sam and Gianna. Kirin nodded then stuffed a chip in her mouth and changed the subject.

"Do you know many people in The Club?'

"A few."

Kirin chose her words carefully. "There's a woman. She's shown interest in Sam. They've been friends since they were kids. And I think she's trying to lure him away."

Stacy balled her fists and hit the table hard, making the bar lady and the man drinking both turn to stare. Kirin sucked down the last sips of her beer then stared through the dark bar haze at the man. Something seemed familiar about him. Then it hit her.

Babyface.

You've. Got. To. Be. Shitting. Me.

Without warning, Kirin jumped up from their booth and stormed between the tables, pushing chairs out of her path like a tornado. She walked straight up to him, empowered by her mostly empty beer, and pushed the tall man off his barstool.

Stacy jumped up and followed, "Kirin, stop!"

"What the hell are you doing here?" Kirin yelled. The young man recoiled from her sudden anger.

"Kirin!" Stacy grabbed her arm, "Stop. He's on our side."

Kirin spun and glared. "Our side? On what planet is *he* on our side? This man hit me over the head with a t-ball bat in my own back yard—knocking me out, broke into my house and threatened me and my kids. He will never be on my side."

Babyface stood. Running from him for so long, and seeing him from afar, she hadn't realized how tall he was. She stepped back instinctively and pushed Stacy behind her.

"What? What do you have to say?" She yelled.

90

"I'm sorry." His voice was almost a whisper. "I followed orders. I never wanted to hurt you or Sam, but I was being controlled by someone else. Please, accept my apology."

Babyface put his hand out. Kirin stared at it like it was a bomb. Stacy walked around her, grabbed Kirin's hand and placed it inside his, holding both as they shook. "Brandon meet Kirin, Kirin—this is my protector—*hired by Sam*—Brandon."

Kirin swallowed hard. Sam had cared enough about her to hire someone to protect her friend. He didn't even know Stacy. She stared openmouthed for a few seconds.

And Babyface had a real name. She shook his hand and stared into his young face. God, was he even old enough to shave? Seeing him this close, he was not only tall, but muscular with deep brown eyes and sandy brown hair. He had a strong jaw and a rock-hard chest under his well-made suit. He had to be in his twenties. He smiled at Stacy and she returned it. His eyes held more than protection. She turned to survey her friend and recognized the look in her eyes. She *liked* him. She knew well enough how hard it was *not* to fall for one's protector.

Stacy turned Kirin's body, steering her back toward their table as Brandon sat back on his bar stool.

"Now where were we…Oh yes, the wretched woman. What was her name?"

"Gianna." Kirin's voice still shook from meeting Brandon.

"Shhhit...you're kidding. Please tell me no."

"Why…you know her?" Kirin leaned forward.

The bar lady walked back over with Stacy's chicken and two more beers. They hadn't ordered the beers, but maybe the woman knew they needed them. She may be in the right business after all.

Stacy took a big gulp of her beer. "She's pretty high up in the hierarchy…several people jump when she says to. Mean as a snake, too. She hates me—partially because I don't take her shit. The woman is arrogant and conceited even with her bigger-than-it-should-be nose. You can't give in to her. Sam will be miserable his whole life if he ends up with her. "

Kirin chewed on the inside of her mouth, "you think they'd still believe you and I are at odds?"

Stacy thought for a moment, "No, my throbbing right eye tells me they know we're speaking."

"Wait, if they have GPS won't they know you're here?"

"Well," Stacy smiled, "my protector over there is like an MIT level techno geek. He's disabled mine and his, so they can't track either of us. He's told them the devices are "glitchy" and that he's ordered new ones, which is a lie. He was assigned after the blast and we've had some lengthy heart to heart talks. He's a cool guy."

"Mm hm," Kirin hummed, raising an eyebrow.

"What?" Stacy grinned and turned to look at him. "Yeah, he's easy on the eyes, too."

Kirin glanced at her phone—it was five after seven. She'd missed another two calls from Sam. Was he waiting at her house? Part of her hoped he was. She hadn't lied to him though—she'd told him she wouldn't be there. Stacy cocked her head to the side.

"Got a date?"

"Nope," Kirin stuffed a chip in her mouth and read an incoming text.

Where are you? We need to talk. Now. Love, Sam

She shook her head, revealing how tipsy she truly was. She didn't have time for love. She needed to convince her friend to come home with her. Kirin glared at the shiner on her eye. Then reached out and grabbed Stacy's hand.

"Right now. Tell me you'll come back. Leave him and everything there. We'll stay up all night and figure out how to keep all of us safe."

Stacy's eyes narrowed. "How the hell are we gonna do that?"

Kirin shrugged, taking another drink. "I don't have a clue. But I will. Wait, what about your brother? Can't he haul these bastards to jail for everything they've done?" she asked.

"Kirin, Steve runs on proof. What proof do we have that they've done anything wrong? So far they've done nothing but threatened harm, not executed it."

"They blew up a hospital cafeteria!"

"Oh, really? And you have some sort of proof? That *they* pulled the trigger?" Stacy's eyes narrowed.

"Well, no, but you and I know they did it." Kirin took another long swig of the fresh beer that their wonderful bar lady brought to them. She would get a fabulous tip as Kirin was feeling perfectly numb.

"Oh, well in that case, let's go arrest them ourselves!" Stacy snorted and popped a piece of chicken in her mouth. She lifted her glass to turn up her beer. She stopped mid sip, staring at the door. Her face drained of all color.

Kirin followed Stacy's line of sight in time to watch two men walk through the door.

Todd and Nicky.

Chapter Sixteen

Stacy moved and darted like an agile cat. She strung her expensive purse around her body and shoved her glittery sunglasses back on her face. The two squinted in the dark then stopped to speak to Brandon. It was obvious from their body language, they weren't happy. Brandon stood when they approached him, towering over both Todd and Nicky. The two men didn't seem intimidated by his size.

Sobered up instantly, Kirin searched the room. She had no escape route where she wouldn't be seen. Shit…if she'd only insisted on carrying a gun, instead of stupid mace. She had no way to protect herself or her friend.

Stacy's hands moved quick and silent. She stacked the plates, condensing them into one pile as if she'd eaten them all herself.

"Get under the table." She commanded in a whisper.

"They'll see me—and my car is outside. They know I'm here!" She shot back.

"They'll kill me for sitting here with you." She stated it matter-of-factly.

"You're positive Brandon is on our side?" Kirin whispered.

Stacy glanced toward him, "Yes, I'm positive."

"Does he carry a gun?"

"Yeah, but he won't pull it on them. He'd be signing his own death sentence."

"Not if he doesn't have a choice."

Stacy narrowed her eyes like Kirin had lost her mind.

"Play along… and figure out a way to signal him to do the same."

Kirin pulled her keys out, with the mace attached, and unsnapped the cover. She held it in her left hand under the table. How accurate would she be with her non-dominant hand, she had no idea, but she had to wait until they were close enough to blind at least one of them.

With her right arm, still in a cast, she turned up the last of her beer. A slow smile crept across Nicky's scarred face as the men stalked toward them. Brandon sat on the edge of his barstool. A horrified look swept across his face. He looked torn like he didn't know which side to root for. She sure hoped Stacy was right.

Todd had changed like someone had given him a style and personality makeover. When was the last time she'd seen him? The dinner party at Stacy's—the night Saul took his life. He'd been nervous back then, to have his father in his home. She now understood why.

Gone was the skinny, slightly hunched guy in dirty jeans and a t-shirt—the one who thought the sun set on Stacy. He'd been replaced by a suited and polished man, whose face had aged ten years in just months. Todd looked taller, more confident and somehow more distinguished.

She guessed inheriting daddy's money and business would do that to a person.

His cheeks were so red, they looked purple in the dark. Murder laced his slight eyes as he looked only at Stacy.

Todd reached the table first. It didn't escape her that Nicky stayed back a few feet, his eyes never wavered from Kirin's face.

Todd glared at Stacy and even with sunglasses on, you could tell she arrogantly stood her ground, staring right back at him.

"Stacy," His voice was even colder. "I thought our conversation the other night *explicitly* detailed you weren't to be around this murderer."

Stacy sat straight, like someone poked her, "We didn't have a *conversation,* Todd, you beat me like a dog and left me lying on the ground."

Todd glanced back toward Nicky, obviously embarrassed that his property was speaking to him in this manner. Nicky crossed his arms and cleared his throat as if to say, "*control her.*"

Todd placed both hands on the table, leaned forward and opened his mouth to speak, again. With zero warning, Stacy cocked her right arm back and punched him in the nose. Stacy screamed from the pain to her hand. Todd stumbled back narrowly missing Nicky and crashing into a chair.

Kirin used the distraction. She bolted from the booth around the outside of the cluster of tables toward Brandon. He stood now, horrified, watching the drama unfold. Nicky darted between tables and caught her a few feet from her target. The stout man tackled her knocking over several tables.

Every ounce of his weight landed directly on her side. Pain ripped where stitches had been just the week before. With quick reflexes, he seized her neck with his thick, wrinkled hands, squeezing. Her vision blurred. Her left hand held the trigger for the mace, but it was useless as he'd pinned down her arms. She couldn't get a clear shot. The evil smile that unfolded told her that not only had he killed this way before, but he'd enjoyed it.

Stacy screamed. Kirin couldn't see what was happening. She didn't want to die this way, on the floor, in a bar, in her favorite green shirt. She tilted her hips knocking him to one side just enough to free her left hand. With God watching over her, she sprayed the mace accurately in both of his eyes, closing her own. Instantly, his hands released her. He rolled off and she moved to the side choking and coughing. They both gasped for air.

Kirin scrambled to her feet. Some of the mace had gotten into her eyes. They stung and burned as she searched for Brandon. She found him making a beeline toward Todd who'd apparently recovered enough to hold Stacy by the waist like a sack of dog food.

Todd yelled for Brandon to come and hold her, so he could teach her a lesson. Kirin sprinted between tables, toward

Brandon. His eyes were locked on Stacy's face. She pulled his gun out of the right-side of his waistband and pointed it at Brandon's face, clicking off the safety.

Brandon spun around glaring like she'd lost her mind.

"Back it up, now!" She yelled. "Down on your knees. Face the door."

The young man glanced from her to Stacy. She prayed Stacy could give him a look and he'd do what she said. With his size, he could disarm her with one hand. He shook his head, then did what she told him to do.

Then, she turned the gun on Todd.

"Let her go." She ordered, through gritted teeth.

"You *will* regret this." He answered.

"Maybe. But you will *never* touch her again." Nicky lay on the ground next to the window, writhing in pain but attempted to sit up. She only had seconds before his anger would enable him to come at her again. She cocked the gun and aimed it straight at Todd's face.

"Now, asshole."

Todd dropped Stacy. She scrambled to her feet, picking up her purse and glasses, crying.

"On the ground scum, face down."

Todd complied.

Kirin walked backward—gun still aimed at Todd and watching Nicky out of the corner of her eye. When she got close enough to the door, she ordered Brandon to stand and open the door.

Stacy laid $200 cash on the bar, mouthing "sorry" to the lady who watched the events unfold through the kitchen window. The lady nodded, as the tip of her shotgun came into view. Kirin had no doubt she'd be smart enough to use it if they came near her. She didn't look as if she needed prodding.

When they crossed the threshold, they ran toward her SUV, climbed in, and peeled out. Kirin shoved the gun in Stacy's hand. Gunshots rang out as their tires screeched out onto the highway, but she was too scared to look back.

Adrenaline coursed through her body, which shook so hard, she had to fight to control the vehicle.

Stacy handed the gun to Brandon in the backseat. She shot her a look. She prayed Stacy knew what she was doing. She pushed her SUV well over the speed limit on every back road she could think of to put distance between them. Brandon touched her arm.

"We need to stop."

"No."

"Kirin, you have to listen to me. They've had transmitters on your vehicle for days. Wherever you run, they can see you. I just thought about it. It's how they found us."

She glanced over at Stacy who nodded as if to say, "trust him." She pulled into the parking lot of an orthodontist office and drove around to the back alley. Screeching to a halt she threw it in park. They all piled out, quick.

Kirin ran to the back, rummaged through her emergency kit until she found a flashlight. Brandon was already on the ground under the vehicle. He snatched the light and shone it along the underbelly of the truck. He pulled off two transmitters. Crawling out, he held out two black boxes.

"This one is ours, but this other one... I don't recognize it. Someone else has been tracking you too."

Fear ran through her. Who else would be tracking her whereabouts?

Just then a dark colored Excursion came barreling down the alley aimed directly at them, at full speed. Brandon pushed Kirin into the backseat, while Stacy jumped into the front seat and Brandon hopped into the driver's seat. He threw the SUV into reverse before her door even clicked shut. The Excursion was on them immediately and rammed into the front of her truck. It jarred them, knocking her around in the backseat like a ragdoll.

The engine roared as Brandon pushed the gas pedal to the floor attempting to outrun them. He swore as he strained to keep the truck straight in reverse. Brandon yelled out as he slammed on the breaks, tires screeching, to avoid hitting a second black SUV parked with no lights on. It blocked their exit.

The force of her truck stopping, threw her body into the floor with her legs and boots still lounging comfortably in the seat. Stacy screamed as masked men jumped out of both SUV's and surrounded their truck, wielding AR rifles and 22's. The men yelled orders and yanked open the doors, shoving guns in their faces.

Kirin scrambled back up on the seat with her legs still stretched out. They were ordered to raise their arms over their heads. They complied.

Then, they heard familiar laughter.

Chapter Seventeen

Two men yanked Brandon out of the driver's seat, slammed him face down on the pavement and cuffed him. Stacy screamed as a tall masked man pulled her from the front seat. Another masked man without a rifle opened the door closest to Kirin's feet. He motioned for her to get out and when she didn't budge, he grabbed her boot with both hands and began to pull, menacing and slow, across the backseat toward the open door.

She wouldn't go down without a fight.

Her heart pounded out of her chest. She let him drag her, hands up until her other boot was free of the seat. Before he could react, she reared back and kicked him in the face as hard as she could. He screamed and yanked his mask off as blood gushed to the ground.

"Woman!" The familiar deep voice yelled, as he dropped her foot and staggered back a few feet.

Her body, which was poised to knock him out and run, stopped short, "Sam?" she cried, raising one hand to her mouth. "Oh my God, is that you?"

"It was…" he said, holding the mask to his nose to stop the bleeding. She could only see him from the eyes up. Was the mist in his eyes from seeing her or simply because he was kicked in the face? He held out his free arm as he exhaled.

"Get over here." He commanded.

Kirin scrambled off the seat and ran to him, knocking him back. He held her and picked her up effortlessly with one arm, holding her tight. Jealous thoughts of where he'd slept the night before, crept back in, but she pushed them away. She'd be happy for the moments they got together. Her arms wrapped around his neck as she kissed his cheek. He smelled of spice and soap and unfortunately, blood. She was alive and so was he.

She may not be for long, but for now, she was.

"*Never* letting you out of my sight, again." He whispered into her hair.

Kirin leaned back and waited for their eyes to meet. She stared for a beat and then said the words she'd been holding back. The ones she couldn't say before but meant with all of her being. "I love you. Truly. And I'm sorry I couldn't say it when you picked me up from the hospital. I felt it, but just couldn't."

Sam's eyes misted again, only this time not from the kick. He grinned at her, then held his lips to her forehead, which was always his sign of truly loving her.

The sound of Stacy sobbing pulled Kirin out of her reunion. Steve Withrow held his sister as she cried. Brandon had been disarmed and placed in the back of the second SUV. Another agent, she didn't recognize, brought the two black boxes to Steve, who promptly took one and stomped it into a pile of plastic then tossed it into the dumpster. He took the other one and threw it into her SUV and twirled one finger in the air signaling everyone to get moving.

"Move out." Steve said.

Sam released her and ran to the driver's side of her SUV. She felt guilty when he pinched his nose, then wiped it to see if the bleeding had stopped. His handsome face was blood stained from his nose to the edge of his ears. Stacy jumped into the back of Kirin's SUV. Her eyes were swollen, but her expression grateful and at ease.

The truck lurched into gear as her seatbelt clicked. Sandwiched between the two black vehicles, they sped down back road after back road. This was her city, but she was so turned around and lost, there was no way she could ever tell another human how to get wherever they were going. They pulled onto a road with woods on both sides.

When they hadn't passed a car in either direction for at least ten minutes, Sam pulled a large phone out of his pocket—a phone she'd never seen—and manually dialed a number.

"Dean? It's time. Keep them safe and underground. My hope is that this won't take longer than a week."

Kirin's heart sank. Her boys and her family would need protection. She was glued to Sam's expression in the dark, illuminated by the instrument panel, as he listened to her Uncle. She swallowed hard.

"No, let Rosa grab Will and take him to school tomorrow, he's got a test. But I'd keep him home the rest of the week. The school has already been notified. Rosa? No she's working on a different project and she's got people watching out for her. I called our friends to the south. They have Maggie and she's having a ball…yours is already there, right? …Good."

Sam glanced over at Kirin and smiled, "Yes sir, always…We love you guys, too."

Sam laid the large phone on the console between them. Tears slid down her cheeks. She turned to look out the window. Sam reached over and intertwined his fingers with hers. His touch alone took her breath away, but she couldn't turn back toward him. Instead she wiped her eyes and turned to look at Stacy. She was curled up in the backseat, sleeping. It was probably the best sleep she'd had in a long time.

Sam lifted her hand in the darkness and kissed it. "Feels like I haven't seen you in weeks and I just saw you this morning." Sam said softly.

"No… it was *yesterday* morning, not this morning. Before the benefit."

Kirin's memory flooded back with such power. Gianna had spent the night with him at the cabin. She pulled her hand away. Jealousy and anger raced around her mind. Sam grabbed it again and squeezed. She glared out her window and shook her head.

"Good try woman, but I saw *you* this morning. I got in about 4am, dropped my angry passenger and her car off at the cabin, got into my car and drove to our house. I slept next to you until about ten 'til six and then remembered I was supposed to meet Chuck. I was late, but he didn't give me too much crap about it. Especially when I told him I'd driven all night to get home."

She jerked her head toward him, "How did you…wait, that's not possible. The alarm didn't register anyone disarmed or rearmed it. I checked. How did you bypass my alarm system?"

"It's simple to bypass that crap alarm. Been doing it for months so I wouldn't wake anyone when I left early or came in late." With the glow of the dash lights, she saw the question clouding his face.

"The bigger question is, why did you check it?" Between glances at the road, he stared deep into her eyes. She stared right back. His green eyes dark. Then she looked down at her boots.

"Gianna answered your phone at the cabin… I assumed… you *stayed* with her. Rosa suggested we check the alarm."

"Ah. That's why you asked me where I slept." His voice was quiet. Angry quiet.

"Yep." She answered. Sam dropped her hand and reached over and touched her chin.

"I told you, Kirin Lane, you are the only woman in my life, didn't I?"

She didn't answer. She'd brought all the doubt, jealousy and worry onto herself. She had nobody to blame. He'd told her not to forget that he loved her, and she'd forgotten at every turn. Sam pulled her face into his and kissed her forehead.

"I love you." He waited, expecting her reply.

"I love you, too." She smiled, not caring, or stopping the tears.

Without moving a muscle, Stacy piped up from the backseat— "Oh for Pete's sake get a room."

Steve's black SUV in the front, suddenly threw on the brakes and skidded to a stop. Then turned right into what could only be described as a hiking trail, not nearly large enough for a regular car, let alone three large SUV's.

Sam shook his head and followed. The other black SUV did the same. Within a minute all three SUV's turned their headlights off with only running lights illuminating the way.

After what seemed like an eternity in eerie pitch blackness, they came upon a blacked-out guard shack. Six men held rifles pointed directly at them, locked and ready. After checking all credentials, they waved all three SUV's through the gate. The forest opened to a primitive air strip illuminated only by the full moon with several short buildings lining the far side of the main runway.

One structure toward the right of the compound looked more like military housing without the landscaping. While another building, toward the middle, looked like offices. One thing that piqued her interest, was that at first glance the structures looked dark, like nobody inhabited them. As they drove closer, she realized the windows were blacked out, but indeed there was life and light inside them.

There were no lights visible anywhere, but squinting just right, she could make out the outline of an intimidating twenty-five-foot wall of what appeared to be barbed fencing. It surrounded the whole place and made it look like an old prison.

Accompanied by FBI agents, they walked into the main office building and down two flights of steps. They were met by four other agents and were introduced to them. Brandon's handcuffs had been taken off. With Sam's explanation, he was no longer being treated as someone from the other side. The sheer amount of technology and computer systems in that one room was staggering.

Something nagged at her in the back of her mind. She looked down at her watch. Nearly ten o'clock. They were searched and forced to hand over all cell phones and technology. Steve explained it was the only clear way they could keep them safe and un-tracked.

Sam, Brandon and Steve met with a group of agents to discuss the raid and next steps. While Stacy and Kirin were escorted to a plain room with nothing inside except a bathroom and two double beds. Stacy suggested to the woman that they'd each need their own room. The agent stared at her and closed the door. They were left to stare at the walls.

Stacy flopped on the bed backwards with her feet up near the pillows and exhaled. "For the first time in eight months, I'm glad Savannah went to live with her dad. I can't imagine how I'd feel trying to get the both of us out of that prison." Stacy's voice quivered at the end.

Kirin sat opposite her on the other bed, "Knowing Savannah, she'd have kicked Todd in the balls and stomped on Nicky's head just for fun."

Stacy laughed with her eyes closed.

"True... too true." Stacy sighed, "Hey?"

"Yeah," Kirin answered. Her head rested on the headboard with her eyes closed.

"Thank you, for saving me."

Kirin's eyes opened, and she glanced over. Stacy's eyes fluttered open, wide and sincere. "Even if we don't make it out of this...I want you to know, you're my best friend and I love you."

Kirin smiled, then shut her eyes again, "We *will* make it out of this. And I love you, too."

"You gotta make me a promise." Stacy sat up on the side of the bed.

"Sure."

"If I'm captured and they haul me back to that place..." Stacy's voice shuddered, "you have to kill me before they do."

Kirin looked at her like she was crazy. Her friend always had a flair for the drama. "It won't come to that."

"*Promise me.* You don't understand the torture these people can inflict. I'd rather be dead. Savannah can live with her dad. Promise me, Kirin."

Kirin closed her eyes and shook her head, "Sure. I'll bring you a 5th of Jack and you can drink yourself to death, how about that?"

Stacy's pointed stare told Kirin she wasn't joking.

Kirin sat up and looked into her friend's eyes. This was important to her. To know she wouldn't have to live as a tortured servant the rest of her life.

"Fine. If it comes to that, sure."

Kirin flopped back and watched her friend. Stacy laid back and closed her eyes, smiling.

~*~

When Kirin woke, Sam was sitting on the edge of her bed, watching her sleep.

"Hey," he whispered, and when she opened her eyes, "We gotta go."

"Where?" she sat up, disoriented.

"Our room, next door. Brandon's gonna take this bed."

"You sure Stacy wants that?" Kirin whispered back and swung her legs to the floor. She rubbed her eyes before opening them fully.

Sam pointed. Stacy and Brandon were locked in an embrace.

"I think she'll be fine with it," he said with one eyebrow up, smirking.

Brandon sat on the side of Stacy's bed holding her while she cried.

Sam led Kirin down the hallway to the next room. It was identical to the one they were just in. Sam walked in behind her, closed the door and locked it.

"You want a bath?" he asked.

"I'd love one." Sam kissed her head then went into the bathroom and started the water.

She took a hard look at herself in the mirror above the dresser. Her shirt sleeve had a few rips in it where Nicky tackled her, and makeup had smeared under her eyes, but in truth she looked no worse for the wear.

"So, fill me in. What happened inside the bar." He raised his voice over the water noise from the bathroom.

She walked over and leaned against the side of the sink, while he scrubbed the blood off his face with a wet washcloth. She recounted the whole experience from Stacy punching

Todd in the face to Kirin spraying mace in Nicky's face as he choked her, to disarming Brandon and their escape.

Sam stood motionless watching her in the mirror, transfixed on her face. Anger mixed with awe washed over him.

"Kirin, what if he'd choked you to death in that bar? We didn't know Todd and Nicola were there until Brandon texted. I couldn't have gotten to you in time if I'd tried." She narrowed her eyes at him, not saying a word.

"Don't get me wrong," he back peddled, "you did really well. I'm just at a loss on what compels you to run *toward* danger…basically unarmed. I'm glad you had the mace but I'm surprised Brandon allowed you to disarm him. Why did you do that?"

Kirin shrugged. "I wanted them to think I forced him to go with us, instead of him going willingly. I didn't want to create yet another target for them to try and hit."

Sam shook his head, smiling. "You can think on your feet, woman, I'll give you that."

The bathtub was full. Sam shut off the water ad laid a clean towel on the sink. Then he wrapped two strong hands around her face, and kissed her long and slow, crushing her upper body into his chest.

"Is it weird that I don't want you out of my sight?"

"No," she smiled, "I can relate."

She pushed him out of the bathroom and shut the door. It wasn't until she peeled off her clothes and reached above her head to tie up her hair that she realized how sore she was from the fight. Stepping gingerly into the steaming water, she allowed her body to relax, and dozed off for a quick nap.

What felt like a few minutes later, Sam tapped on the door, "Honey, it's almost midnight—dry off and I'll put you to bed and take my shower."

Midnight…shit. She washed her body, dried off and put her clothes back on. When she opened the door, Sam stood in the doorway, smiling.

"What?" She asked, kissing him on the cheek as she walked past.

"They brought a stack of clean clothes. Rummage through and see what you can find to wear to bed…or wear the pretty green top," he said, his voice seductive, and a glimmer in his eye, "or nothing…you know, whatever you want." He grinned as he closed the bathroom door behind him.

When she heard the shower start, she yanked her boots on and darted toward the door. She waffled—should she leave the door unlocked so she could sneak back in, or lock it? Unlocked would leave him unprotected in the shower and she couldn't do that. She grabbed a cup sitting on the dresser. She'd say she was going for ice. She'd memorized the wench's cell number, now to find a phone.

Kirin jogged down a plain colored hallway until she found a stairwell. Taking the steps two at a time as silently as she could, she opened the door on the bottom floor, a crack. She needed to find Steve. She'd have to talk him out of a phone. She shook her head. Wet hair stuck to her back. What she really needed was a plan, but nothing was coming. She and Sam were safe inside the fortress, but what about her boys. Nicky's beady eyes flashed in her memory. The thought of his thick fingers squeezing the life out of Will and Little Jack catapulted her forward. This wasn't about her safety, it was about theirs.

Pushing the door open a few inches wider, she realized it was a side door leading into a large round room. Command central. Long tables cut through the center of the room adorned with screens. Men and women in uniform crawled all around. Movement caught her eye. Just to the right of the door, she could make out the outline of a guard, holding a rifle. He hadn't noticed the door as his eyes were trained on two men arguing. She followed his line of sight.

Steve stood toe to toe with a husky man with thick, dark hair. The exchange looked heated. The noise in the room doubled and both men ran toward a screen. The guard stepped a few feet toward them, allowing her to push open the door more. She strained to hear the conversation.

"Sir! The shipment is complete, personnel are on the ground ready to intercept." A male officer yelled out.

"Affirmative," Steve barked. "How many girls?"

"Six, sir."

"They're getting ballsy transporting so many." Steve switched his gaze to a different screen. "Location of target?" He squinted toward one screen.

"Not on location, sir."

Steve turned and walked around the man, shaking his head, "No. Turner, I said no…We're not going to risk her life."

The man turned on his heel and followed Steve, arguing his point, "You know it's the only way we're gonna get him out in the open, sir. He came out tonight *for her* and the last time our cameras spotted him was inside the cafeteria, because *she* was there. He'll go back into hiding and we won't be able to get near him if we don't strike now."

They were talking about *her*…Kirin's mind kicked into gear. She needed their help and they needed hers.

She took a deep breath and opened the door. Shoulders back she marched toward Steve. She didn't make it more than a foot into the room before armed guards surrounded her. Two rifles pointed at her head as two men yelled for her to stop. They apparently didn't like to be surprised.

Steve yelled, "Stand down, she's a civilian guest." The guards withdrew their guns. Steve cast glares at the two guards, probably for letting a civilian get the drop on them. They each turned on their heels and walked back to guard the door.

"Kirin, what the hell are you doing down here…everything okay?" he said, wrapping an arm around her. The man he called Turner sauntered over then stared at her like he wanted to say something.

The large clock on the wall read 11:55 pm. She had only five minutes to convince them she needed a phone. She bypassed Steve and stuck out a hand to Turner, who immediately took it.

"I'm Kirin."

"John. John Turner. Nice to meet you."

She turned to Steve, "He's right, you know."

Steve looked at John then leveled a look at her. "About what?"

"The only way that you're gonna get him out in the open, is if you use me for bait."

John looked like he could burst. He smiled, slapping Steve on the back. "You were right, she's smart too. Hell yeah! This is gonna work, we're gonna finally catch this son of a bitch."

Steve shook his head at them both. Glaring pointedly at her. "I said no. I can't do that. And besides, Sam isn't going to stand for this."

"Sam won't know, because you won't tell him." She said assertively.

"And what makes you think that?" Steve shifted his weight, angrily.

"Because you know deep down, just like I do, that Turner's right. You need me and I need something from you, so we're gonna make a deal."

Steve stepped back, crossing his arms over his chest with his head cocked to the side. "I'm listening."

"I'll be the bait, as long as you promise me two things and grant me one favor."

Steve furrowed his brow, "What?"

"First, I need a phone… one that can't be traced. And I need it in the next two minutes. I have to make a call before midnight."

Steve narrowed his eyes, but she kept talking. "And secondly, you have to promise that you won't tell Sam the plan until it's too late to stop it. And you'll protect *him*, not me, no matter what."

Steve exhaled, and shook his head. "This isn't regulation. They could have my ass for enlisting a civilian." The struggle between winning and following rules washed over his face.

110

"This is dangerous, Kirin. They might take one look at you and shoot you in the head. No words, just retribution. That's how they live. We wouldn't have time to save you."

"Steve, I have one minute to make that call. You have one minute to make the right choice. End them. End the drug smuggling, the human trafficking, the murder, kidnappings, and the terror, forever. You're the FBI for crying out loud. He won't get anywhere near me, right?" She spoke to John, hoping he'd concur.

John shook his head vigorously, "She's right Withrow, we wouldn't allow her out of our sight. Plus we have our ace in the hole on the inside."

Steve looked at his shoes and then produced his phone, handing it over.

Kirin put her cup on the floor and snatched the phone out of his hands to dial the number. He wouldn't let her out of arm's reach while she made the call. He stood over her as the phone rang.

When the smug woman answered, Kirin said the one word that would save her boys and the man they both loved...

"Yes."

Chapter Eighteen

She pressed the end button and handed it back to Steve. His eyebrows shot up when he saw that her hand trembled. John Turner trotted away, happy. Steve shoved the phone back in his side pocket and stared at her, trying to work out what she'd done.

Her gut churned and it took everything she had not to cry. She'd set this plan in motion to save him, but she'd have to hurt him to do it. Her goal was to get some assurance that if the FBI failed, Sam would live. She got what she needed, but the thought of *her* being with him for the rest of his life made her ill.

She'd rolled the slow-motion bowling ball down the shiny lane and now could only stand back and watch it hit the pins.

She swallowed back the lump in her throat and spoke.

"Think you could do one more favor?"

Steve hitched an eyebrow that said she'd about run out of favors.

"Think you could do some acting? Pretend...at the right moment," she swallowed hard, "we're in love?"

His eyes grew wide and he took a small step toward her and into her space. Steve lowered his voice. "Why? You guys having problems?"

"Yes or no?" Her body and mind were exhausted. She couldn't tell him why. He stared at her. His lips turned up slightly.

"I could manage that. But you'd have to give me a good reason."

She ignored that part, "And you can't tell Sam it's not genuine."

"I won't lie to him." His stare reached her soul as he took her hands in his. He was honest and serious. Who had she become, that using a man who she now suspected had feelings for her was a good idea?

She took a tiny step back. "If it's too much to ask, I could see if Turner would do it."

Steve glared in John's direction and without missing a beat he answered, "No."

Sam burst through the door, wet headed and angry. His terrified gaze darted about the room, falling on her and Steve, and their intertwined hands. The two guards pounced on his intrusion quicker than the last time. Steve dropped her hand and called them off.

Sam marched toward them, red-faced and sizing them both up, he stared from her to Steve. She was fairly sure he'd been bitten by the same jealousy bug she'd been trying to kill all week.

Steve's poker face stayed strong, but he didn't speak, so she picked up her cup from the floor and began.

"I came down here to get some ice and stumbled into this room. I was greeted with rifles shoved in my face too."

Steve nodded.

"Good shower?" She turned on her best smile, and walked toward Sam.

His shoulders relaxed slightly, but that handsome face still held doubt. She placed her arms around him and kissed his cheek, burying her head. He smelled of soap and Sam. Mixed, it was her most favorite smell. And she'd have to give it up soon.

Sam wrapped strong arms around her and squeezed. She could feel him mouth something to Steve over her head. They walked back through the door and started up the stairs.

"Kirin…" Sam stopped on the third step and grabbed her hand then continued, "until this shit is over don't leave without at least giving me a heads up. I flipped out, thinking someone had taken you."

Kirin glanced at her shoes, then back at him. She hadn't thought about how he'd feel. This was going to be hard for them both, but especially him. For the first time in his life, he'd allowed himself love and she'd have to break his heart to get him to leave. Tears filled her eyes, overwhelmed with the thought of giving him up. It took all she had not to divulge her plan right there, but she knew it wouldn't help the ones she was trying to protect.

When they reached their room, Kirin spoke. "Can you remember one thing for me?" She waited for their eyes to meet, then continued, "no matter what happens, you will always be the love of my life."

Sam nodded, but his eyes narrowed like he was figuring out a puzzle as he opened the door. He sat on the bed and removed his shoes. He watched her every move. He undressed and laid his clothes on a chair next to the bed. Climbing into bed, he groaned. It'd been a taxing day on them both and her heart filled with a strong desire to comfort him.

She turned out the light and undressed, opting not to wear the green top, nor the clothes on the dresser.

Climbing into bed she found Sam's mouth as he wrapped arms around her, warming her from the inside out.

This was the last time, she told herself. She tried to engrain into her memory every touch, every kiss, every shudder, and every feeling. Her memory would be all she had once he was gone.

~*~

The next morning, she woke to an empty bed. The room was cold with no Sam heater next to her. She pulled the blanket up around her neck. When her bladder screamed, she jumped up and scavenged through the clothes to find a pair of military utility pants, socks, men's underwear and a navy-blue t-shirt. She even found a pair of work boots in her size that would work. Kirin scooped everything up and ran to the bathroom. The clothing was a little large, but at least it was warm. She found an oversized lightweight hoodie in the closet and laid it out just in case.

She brushed her hair back using her fingers and found a hair tie in the bathroom. When she splashed water on her face, she heard Stacy's voice in the next room. She turned off the water and strained to hear her.

"It's suicide," Her voice was shrill and panicky. "They have the compound locked up tight and with the way things went down last night, there's no way I could get us back in."

A man's muffled voice floated through the wall, but she couldn't make out the words. Stacy's high pitched, loudness came through just fine.

"...Yes, but she doesn't stay there...the other two do, but she cats around at night, you know that."

Gianna. She cats around, she's a...

With a click, the door swung open, startling her. Sam carried two coffees and a bag of something that smelled warm and sugary. Her stomach growled on cue. Her chips and salsa at the bar had done little for her the night before.

Sam grinned, his green eyes gleaming. Last night's late exercise had energized him, it seemed.

"Morning, my love."

With his hands full, she had a great opportunity to kiss his face, and he could do nothing about it. She grabbed his face, kissing him deeply.

When she pulled back, Sam set the coffees and food on the table, and stepped back. His face looked puzzled, mixed with a little accusation.

"Why do your kisses feel like goodbyes?" He said, eyeballing her. "Please tell me you aren't planning something really stupid, here?" He waited for a reply, but clearly didn't expect one.

"Kirin, the FBI are so close to taking them down. Trained officers will go in and get them and with last night's mainly successful raid, they've crippled them once again. It won't be long. They have enough evidence to storm the place and put them behind bars. Then we can go home and feel safe."

She pointed toward the coffee and he nodded, "What do you mean, *mainly* successful?"

Sam seized his coffee and chose the chair next to the desk. "They captured one of our guys." He took a sip and stared down at the worn carpet.

"They've sent word they'd execute anyone who meddled in their drug business. Last night's raid cost them dearly and their hive is buzzing with anger right now. Let *them* do the work, Kirin, we're just here to stay safe."

"You're not going with them to apprehend Todd? He's the leader, right? What about Gianna? Where does she think you are?"

Sam exhaled, "Todd's just a pawn. Steve thinks Nicky is calling the shots, but there's someone else involved too. They aren't quite sure who it would be. Truth be told, Todd should rightfully be the leader since it passes from father to Son, but he doesn't have the stomach for the job. He only treated Stacy like that because Nicky manipulated him."

Her mind twitched to attention. "Sam, are Nicky and Gianna related?"

Sam's eyes narrowed, "Yeah, why?"

You don't think Nicky is trying to push Todd out and Gianna in do you?"

Sam stared at her. His eyes told her he'd thought the same thing. But he shook his head, "She doesn't want it. She wants to go back to high society in Cleveland and be done with all of this."

And take you with her.

"You sure?" she asked, searching his face.

"No. But I know she's hated Nicky since we were kids. I don't think that fact has changed."

She took a long sip of her coffee. If the FBI was after Nicky, but in truth Gianna ran the show, then they weren't tracking the right person. And if Kirin could put this together, surely the FBI had figured it out.

Sam opened the bag and handed her a breakfast sandwich. She took it gratefully. He watched her.

"I want to ask you something serious, and I need an honest answer."

"Awfully deep for eight in the morning," Kirin smiled, unwrapped her sandwich and took a huge bite.

Sam grinned, "I need to know you're still with me."

Kirin stopped chewing, "What do you mean?"

"This thrilling and dangerous side of our lives is almost over. You haven't mentioned wedding plans in a long time. Has all this... baggage, made you change your mind?" He set his sandwich down. "Now that you're aware of what I am, or what I *was,* have your feelings changed? Feels like you're planning to leave."

She set her sandwich down, stood, and walked toward him, with her hands on her hips.

"What did I tell you last night? And what happened right there?" she gestured toward the bed. "Was I the only one that felt that? I don't care what you did in The Club...it makes no difference to me if you parked cars, broke thumbs, or killed people. You were forced to do things you didn't want to do. You are who you are and you're mine." She spoke from the heart, and clearly her heart wasn't accepting the fact she'd be letting him go very soon.

She sat on his outstretched leg and continued, "Wedding plans aren't on my mind right now, because surviving is."

Sam pulled her into his chest.

It was at that moment, the idea hit her. Her stomach twisted thinking about it. She'd have to hurt him in the worst way for him to turn loose of her.

She knew deep down what to do.

Chapter Nineteen

When Sam retreated to the bathroom, she picked up his new phone from the dresser. It was the same type Steve had handed her the night before. She couldn't help but pick it up and look for texts between him and *her*. She had to know.

The rushing water of the toilet flushing moved her fingers faster. Then, water in the sink turned on.

The texts started from her,

"Sammy, have you considered my offer?"

"Not happening, G" He'd written back.

She hated the familiarity in their banter. Gianna had known him twenty years longer, but that didn't stop the jealous monster from rising inside Kirin.

"They'd all be safe. One night. Come on, we both know you've done it for money, let's do it for fun. Get out of that prison and meet me. Two hours tops."

He hadn't seen the last text as it'd just come through. She laid the phone back on the dresser at the same moment Sam emerged from the bathroom.

She tried her best not to look guilty, swallowed hard and stood, "I'm gonna check on Stacy. Where are you going today?"

Sam watched her carefully for a few seconds then shrugged it off, "To find Steve. See if they rescued the agent who was captured. Meet back for lunch?" She nodded. Sam kissed her forehead, grabbed up his phone and shut the door behind him.

She finished her coffee, and tidied up the room, all the while planning how to break up with him. She choked back tears more than once. Drying it all up, she shut her door and walked to Stacy's room.

"Come in," Stacy sang, sounding chipper.

"Good morning, sunshine. You're *awake* this morning." Kirin narrowed her eyes, smiling at her friend as she shut the door behind her. Stacy's face glowed.

"Yep. A full night's sleep outside the fortress." She flitted about the room straightening and cleaning. Both the beds had been slept in. Maybe nothing happened. It wouldn't surprise her if Brandon was a gentleman.

"Where's Babyface?" Kirin sat in one of the hardback chairs.

Stacy rose from picking something off the ground and stared. "Who?"

"Brandon."

Stacy's smile spread across her face. "I'll tell him you call him that, he'll find humor in the irony. He's downstairs in some stupid, super-secret meeting."

Stacy watched her, her face losing all humor. "What's the matter?"

Kirin took a deep breath. "Can we talk?"

Stacy stopped flitting around the room and plopped onto one of the newly made beds and waited while Kirin gathered her thoughts.

"I'm afraid the only way you and I are gonna survive is if Todd and Nicky are *gone*." She let it sink in, then continued. "And I know you. Part of you still loves Todd. If he's killed or put away for life, how's that gonna affect you?"

Stacy stopped fidgeting for a second and stared. Her expression was an odd mixture of sadness that turned to fear. Stacy stared out the window at the grey clouds looming outside, then sighed deep.

"I don't know. I haven't accepted he's no longer *my* Todd. Before…he was caring, loving and comical. Endearingly vulnerable. And looking back, he was jittery around his family—of course now, I understand why." Stacy stared at her hands as a tear ran down one cheek. Kirin left her chair, sat on the bed and grabbed her friends' hands. Stacy's head snapped up to look into Kirin's eyes.

"They're all monsters." Stacy whispered, her eyes fearful. "You don't know how many times, I had to listen to someone beg for their life inside that mansion. The dungeon-like basement must be where they keep people before they die, but it's also where the heat system is. I used to shove towels inside the vents in my room to block out the screams, but then I'd get cold. I spent hours hiding in that room with noise cancelling headphones on."

There was a longing in her voice. It was as if she wished she could've done more than just hide. Something told Kirin she'd need more information about this place.

"Did you ever go down there?"

"No, never. To be honest the fortress is so huge, I'm not even sure which set of stairs lead there. But I know that's where they take certain people. People that don't ever seem to come back. I once heard a woman crying down there. From the sounds...they did awful things to her before they killed her. I sat awake all night. Even tried to find the stairs that night but couldn't. That's what scares me the most."

A fine mist pelted the window and for a moment, it mesmerized her. Kirin stood and walked to it. She had to think of a way out of this. They needed Todd and Nicky gone. For that matter Gianna too. But for now, they needed to be off their radar.

Other than retribution, what did they gain from killing Stacy and Kirin? Gianna wanted Kirin out of the picture, so having her killed was the easiest way to win Sam. But why Stacy? If Todd truly loved Stacy, he wouldn't let Nicky do that, right?

Todd was being bullied by Nicky into being someone he wasn't, but she still couldn't trust him to save Stacy. He'd hit Stacy behind closed doors to show the family he wasn't weak. That wasn't someone who loved her, that was a coward with a mean streak.

What had Nicky said when she was in the hospital?

"...what is important is that you tell that fiancé of yours to stop meddling in my business or let's just say I will give new

120

meaning to your upcoming wedding vows of 'til death do us part."

What did she know about their *"business?"* Sam had said they'd used him and Gianna to get "property and things" The Club wanted. And when Steve had visited her in the hospital, he'd spoken of a shipment of "girls." She needed to know what else they were peddling.

Kirin shuddered, "Let's go for a walk and stretch our legs—want to?"

"Sure. I could use some fresh air." Stacy stood and drug on tennis shoes she found in the closet.

They walked outside just as they'd come in. Free. Officers were everywhere, but they only observed. Nobody tried to stop them. Steve must've briefed his officers that civilians would be milling about, because this time no guns were shoved in their faces.

October sun warmed their backs as they headed west toward a row of airplane hangars. They walked along a working, but dilapidated runway, rather than twist an ankle in the knotted grass. They talked more like two neighbors taking a walk than people plotting to stay alive.

The last metal airplane hangar in line had its big bay door open with a dump truck backed into it, while the others all looked abandoned and shut. The windows in the first few they'd passed were way too high to see what was inside, so out of curiosity, they headed for the last one.

About fifty yards from the door, two officers, dressed in drab green with automatic weapons jogged toward them. "Stop!" One of them yelled.

Both ladies complied. The officers reached them but stood cautiously a few feet away. "This area is off limits. Please head back to the barracks."

Stacy's demeanor changed instantly. Her smile wattage doubled as she kick-started her charm. "Guys listen—we're all on the same side! We only wanted to look inside one of these giant hangars. I've never been inside one before—have you, Kirin?"

Oh, Lord. Kirin wasn't good at feigning innocence or sounding like a helpless female and Stacy knew it. But her friend put her on the spot, so she had to try.

"Uh, no... No, I haven't. You can't grasp how big they are without standing inside. We won't touch anything, I promise." She added, smiling. Her tone was so sickly sweet and high, she had a hard time pulling it off without laughing.

The older of the two officers narrowed dark eyes at them but continued his polite smile. "Commander Withrow has given us direct orders that nobody gets in there, *especially* civilians."

Stacy grinned wide, "and being commander Withrow's sister, he knows how much I like architecture, so I promise he wouldn't mind."

Architecture? Kirin had to clear her throat to hide the giggle. She piped up, "Can't we just stand at the edge and peek in?" The younger officer's face softened. He seemed affected by their charms, but the older gentleman wasn't buying it.

"Impossible, Ms. Lane. Please go back to the barracks and enjoy your stay."

He knew exactly who they were. They'd need to change tactics to get a gander.

"Okay, thanks." She turned on her heel, linking arms with Stacy.

Stacy looked straight ahead and spoke. "Giving up?"

"For now...we'll come back later, when crusty there takes a break." Kirin's eyebrows danced as Stacy nodded and smiled.

They'd walked less than a hundred feet, when piercing sirens rang out overhead that paralyzed them both. Kirin held her ears. A small grey plane flew toward the runway. Officers seemed to pour out of every door, like roaches. She squinted toward it. It looked unmanned and too small to be real, more like a large toy.

Stacy and Kirin were grabbed from behind by the same two green suited officers and led toward the hangar they'd wanted to see. As they were ushered inside, she got a quick look around.

She now knew why they didn't want her snooping around.

The space was industrial, filled with concrete floors and metal siding and it reeked of jet fuel. It stung her lungs and permeated the large space, but there was no jet inside. The space was so jam packed with boxes marked "Prescription" and bags of white powder, they couldn't have parked a bicycle inside.

This was the mother lode of drugs. Hundreds of billions of dollars' worth of drugs. She suspected that the other hangars were just as full. No wonder The Club wanted them dead. They'd stolen one of their sources of income.

The older man ushered them down a narrow set of concrete steps that lead nowhere. They were basically inside a cement foxhole. As other officers scrambled around above ground, they were escorted to the very back of the hallway and told to crouch down in a shadow by a gruff talking, dark haired, female officer gripping a handgun. According to her tag, Martinez was her name.

As they'd been led downstairs, Kirin glanced back. Officers scurried to close the main hangar door. One man tinkered with a box on the wall as the other officers yanked on the door itself. It was stuck. The lights flickered. Noise inside was deafening, peppered with officers who yelled out orders and explosions down the runway. Men fired what looked like handheld rockets from the open door at two giant black attack helicopters.

From their vantage point, she could see the entire sky was lit up with orange fire and black smoke.

She watched in horror as something caught on fire and exploded on the other side of the runway. It looked like one of the SUV's that had saved them the night before.

She prayed Sam was safe.

Chapter Twenty

From their crouched position, she watched as smoke engulfed the hangar. Surely, the stacked boxes of white powder were highly flammable. If the fire reached them, they'd know *intimately* how deadly drugs could be.

A blacked-out van screeched to a halt just to the right of the large bay door. Gunfire ensued. Kirin's legs began to shake. She'd crouched too long. If they needed to run, her legs wouldn't respond. She stood and pulled a terrified looking Stacy to her feet. Both ladies held their ears and Stacy shot Kirin a look of terror.

The van held soldiers. Lots of them, dressed all in black with only their eyes showing and brandishing weapons. They poured out of the van like water, running in every direction. The sound of gunshots doubled.

Kirin glanced around. They'd be shot like fish in a barrel in the alcove where they stood. Officer Martinez had a tattoo that led from her neck, down her back and disappeared down the collar of her uniform. She stood in a wide stance with her gun, rock solid, pointed outward toward the stairs to blow away anyone who came down. Kirin yelled toward her.

"We have to move."

The woman shook her head. "My orders are to stay."

Kirin grabbed the woman's arm and yanked, spinning the woman's body toward them. "We're gonna die, if we stay."

She had a pretty face, natural red lips and deep-set brown eyes—eyes that now told Kirin she wasn't taking orders from her. Their noses almost touched as the officer glared and yelled back. "We're *not* leaving."

Just then, the backside of a green suited officer appeared at the top of the steps. He fired his rifle but was overtaken. His body careened backwards and tumbled awkwardly down into their alcove with arms and legs twisting unnaturally. He was dead, and they were next. Kirin turned to face Stacy. Stacy stared at the unmoving body at their feet. Kirin shook her friend until their eyes met. She nodded upward. Stacy followed her line of sight and nodded back.

Interlacing her fingers, she hoisted Stacy up toward the railing above them. Stacy was tall enough to grab hold of the metal rungs and began pulling herself up. Stacy's scream pierced the noise as two hands grabbed her under the arms and began pulling her upward. Kirin snatched one of Stacy's ankles until she saw Brandon's red face and Stacy grabbing at him like a parched human finding water in a desert.

Two masked thugs, one much larger than the other, with rifles in hand crept down the steps toward Kirin and Martinez. The woman backed up, pinning Kirin's body against the back wall. Protecting her. Overwhelming sympathy rose in Kirin's chest. This woman was prepared to die for her. And she didn't even know her.

Both men aimed rifles at the woman's face, but they didn't shoot. Then it clicked. They must've been ordered to take Kirin alive. And they didn't want to screw that up by shooting this woman in the head. Whoever wanted her dead, wanted to do it themselves. Maybe she could keep this woman alive, but she'd have to take a risk. God, she hoped she was right.

By now the men were at the bottom of the steps and came to a halt. Over the noise, she yelled, "You want me? She lives."

The female officer's head cocked to one side. She cut her eyes briefly back at Kirin, not moving her stance, as if to say Kirin had lost her mind. Kirin used the slight hesitation to hip shove the woman off balance. She staggered just enough for Kirin to grab and yank the handgun from her, spinning it to rest underneath her own chin. The larger of the black hooded men flinched. When the female officer caught herself, she turned back toward Kirin and stopped.

"What the…" Her jaw tightened. Her angry face made Kirin doubt she'd done the right thing. Each of the men before them had a rifle pointed at a different woman's head. Kirin repeated.

"You want me alive, you let her live."

The bigger one, lowered his gun. Without warning, he punched the woman soldier in the jaw. She fell to the ground with a sickening thud. She lay motionless but breathing—alive, but out cold.

Then he turned and held out one hand for her gun. She didn't have another option. She could possibly take one of them out, but she'd die in the process. Who'd protect her boys then? Sam maybe? Assuming he was still alive. Reluctantly, she handed over the pistol.

Her only thought was, at least Stacy got away.

The larger man snatched the pistol and stuck it in the back of his pants, then grabbed Kirin's arms and yanked them hard behind her back, cuffing her. The other masked man produced a black bag, hooded her, then led her up the steps.

She felt like a dog who'd never walked on a leash before. She tilted and staggered. From underneath the hood, she could see her feet which helped a little. One man held her tight across the back of her neck, while the other held her elbow, high, making her shoulder burn. She was a criminal in their world. Someone who'd killed their president. Or so they thought.

Shots rang out. She prayed she'd be hit by a stray bullet. At least then, they might just drop her, thinking she was dead or too much trouble. No such luck. The light surrounding her feet changed from dark gas-soaked concrete to light-gray pointy gravel. They'd ushered her outside. Sunlight filtered through the black hood, allowing her to see objects in shadow. A giant truck roared into the hangar. Black suited bodies scurried and dodged bullets to load boxes of drugs into the back of the truck.

As the two men ushered her, a realization smacked her in the face. If they took her, she was dead. Sam would never find her. They'd been looking for The Club's fortress for weeks. Her gut twisted.

The men led her, zig-zag style around bodies littering the ground. The gunfire had slowed, but not ceased. She focused on dragging her feet and looking at faces. Please don't let any of them be Sam. She had to force her eyes to stay open and scan the ground. There were so many. This couldn't be real.

Death surrounded her. Not *because* of her, she told herself. They came for the stolen drugs too. But she couldn't deny, they came for her too.

A diesel engine ahead roared to life. And they were headed straight for it. Through the hood, she made out a large, urban assault vehicle, with huge tires and four doors. She dug in, dragging her feet like a dog who knows he's going to the vet. She pulled backward with everything she had, twisting and kicking, but the man holding her elbow lifted higher on her bad arm. Pain shot through her shoulder. They held her so high only her tiptoes were touching the ground. One man's grip indicated he'd rather just shoot her in the head and be done.

The smaller man opened the back door, while the other one lifted her and chucked her inside. She skidded to a halt on her face, the seatbelt scraping her cheek.

The sting of blood rushing to the surface gave her a realization. These animals didn't care if they injured her, they just couldn't deliver her dead. Trying to sit up, she felt like a duck with broken wings trying to right herself on the seat. Idly, she wondered if they'd put a seatbelt on her. Ridiculous. It'd be like taking the time to wrap eggs in bubble wrap before egging someone's house. She was set to die anyway. Bruises wouldn't hurt.

Before the door closed, she spotted a body in the gravel. The face, once she recognized it, trapped her gaze. She couldn't look away. Was he dead? She couldn't tell.

Brandon's eyes were closed. His face was pale and littered with dirty pieces of gravel. His babyface features somehow looked older. Her heart sank for the boy. And if they killed him, they had Stacy. Todd would torture her. The thought sent angry electricity through her. She had one friend in a coma, and one headed toward torture. They'd all been through enough. The image of Stacy's purple eye came into clear focus.

Kirin used her cuffed hands to push off the back seat and sit straighter. With her head hanging low, she stared under the hood at the military boots she'd been given. One of the thugs climbed in next to her tossing a black bag in the floorboard. Kirin angled her body toward him slow, then counted to three in her head. Quick as lightning, she planted her left foot and kicked up toward his head with the full force of her right leg.

She tagged him in the nose, but not as hard as she'd hoped. He let out a yelp, grabbed her by the leg and shoved her body into the floorboard. Kirin kicked like an angry child throwing a fit. Her heavy boots pummeled his knees, shins and even stubbed one of his outstretched fingers as he tried to grab her legs to stop her. Curse words flew out of the man as he scrambled and yelled.

The man in the front seat had no sooner sat, then he'd thrown the car into drive and sped down the runway. He cursed as he swerved around vehicles on fire, ripping off his mask and throwing it in the floor. He was young. God, he still had peach fuzz on his cheeks. Gunshots peppered the door next to Kirin. The sound alone caused her to stop kicking and her eyes to shut. She was damn lucky she hadn't been hit by a stray bullet.

From the floorboard, it felt like they were going a hundred miles an hour. The truck creaked and bounced. The young driver yelled, "Hold on!" In an instant the sound of crushing metal filled the cab. The truck pitched and flew airborne before bouncing and crashing back to the ground.

The fence. He'd broken through the fence. Something inside her snapped. There'd be no way Sam could find her now—if he was still alive. Her heart sank, and she was glad they couldn't see her face. Hot tears formed. Neither Sam nor the FBI would be swooping in at the last minute to save her this time.

Nope. If she wanted to survive, she was going to have to use her wits. And do it alone.

Chapter Twenty-One

If she'd been the sort to get carsick, now would be the opportune moment. The driver swerved in and out of the narrow one-lane road. The screeching sound of trees scraping the side of the truck, made her wish her arms were free so she could cover her ears.

The man in the back seat pulled off her hood. Sunlight flooded her vision, causing her to squint. Then he ripped off his ski mask and slapped it to the back of his neck. One of the stray bullets had grazed him and it bled like a fountain. With his free hand he pointed at her.

"Kick me again, Lane, and I swear to God I'll knock you out."

She nodded. His voice was low and robust. It matched his body. He eyed her as he unzipped his bag and dug around. She watched him struggle. Something about him seemed familiar. His nose maybe? He was a stout man, probably in his thirties, with round, piercing dark eyes and a strong, stubble-lined jaw. The ski mask had jacked-up his hair, making him look not only murderous, but bat-crap crazy. His lips pursed as he searched in the bag, looking over at her every few seconds like he was too close to a copperhead about to strike.

He pulled out a first aid kit but couldn't open it with one hand. He tried turning it on its side and propping it against one leg, yanking on the clasp. It wouldn't open. He even resorted to using his boots to pull it apart but couldn't get it to open.

Finally, she spoke. "Take these cuffs off and I'll help."

He slid her a look of not no, but Hell no.

"Have it your way. You're gonna bleed out. I'm a nurse, you know."

He searched her face, then shook his head and leaned toward the front.

"Child-locks engaged, right?"

The younger man nodded as he navigated the large vehicle onto the main road. The truck bounced, and the tires squealed, changing from gravel to pavement. Then it leveled out. From where she sat, she could only see trees whizzing by. She couldn't see if anyone followed but based upon her captors face when he turned to look for himself, there was nobody there.

Of course not.

"Move up." He ordered.

Her knees were shoved next to her nose and her hands were still cuffed behind her. What the hell did he expect her to do, float from the floorboard to the seat? She prayed the door didn't accidentally open, or at this speed, she'd be roadkill. Pressing her back against the door, she shoved her body upward, grunting. Her boots gripped the carpet, which helped her to get into a squatting position. Her movements were slow, but her body was rising. Her thighs quivered trying to use her own body weight to heave herself on to the seat.

Impatient, the man reached out effortlessly with his free hand, grabbed her by the elbow and threw her onto the seat. She turned and glared. He glared right back. Pulling a carabiner off his belt loaded with keys, he flipped them around until he found the right one.

"Turn." He ordered, and she complied. Grabbing her elbow once more he pulled her back roughly to get close enough to unlock her cuffs. Before turning the key, he leaned forward and lowered his voice.

"Don't do anything stupid."

When the cuffs released, she pulled her aching arms around and rubbed her wrists. His eyebrows shot up as if to say, get on with it.

Kirin grabbed the first aid box between them and popped it open. Raising her eyebrows as if to say, wow, that was hard. The man rolled his eyes.

She angled her body toward his. Her expert, nimble fingers took out tape, gauze, some large bandages and a few alcohol swabs. She opened the bandages and ripped a few pieces of tape. He watched her every move. When she tore open the alcohol swabs, she raised one and waited. He nodded. Pulling his hand and a blood-soaked mask away from the wound, she rubbed the small fabric over the wound. The man's body went rigid with pain.

"Mother scratcher!" He yelled, causing her to stop and stare at him.

"What?" he yelled over the road noise.

"Nothing." She giggled. "Just never heard that one, *out of an adult*, that's all." She pulled out another swab and applied it. Then to herself, but loud enough he could hear, "Next, he'll be saying, 'whoops-a-daisy.'"

His eyes narrowed. With one hand, she turned his head toward the window, giving her a better look at the wound. No bullet. In a perfect world, he'd need stitches. She'd found two butterfly bandages, she hoped would close it. She dabbed at the running blood with some gauze, then applied the butterflies, gauze, tape and one more bandage. When she finished, she gathered the wrappers.

He turned back toward her, his hand touching the bandages. His expression was still angry, but in his eyes she noticed a touch of gratefulness. He grabbed the trash from her hands and shoved it and the first aid kit into his bag. Before he zipped it, she caught a glimpse of rope and something shiny, a knife maybe.

She scooted back and stared out the window. She'd lived here most of her life, but honestly had no idea where they were. A clicking sound made her turn and look back at her captor.

When their eyes met, he ordered, "seatbelt." For once, she didn't argue.

"So," she began, even though he shot her a look like she'd lost her mind, "you from around here?"

He shook his head to himself, then leaned forward toward the driver. "How long?"

"An hour before we ditch the truck to go in the back way. Think they were smart enough to tag a tracer?"

"No." The man in the backseat answered. His knee began to bounce as he checked his watch and spoke only to the man up front.

"Cutting it too close."

The driver nodded, then added, "Joel—you see team two? They get their target and make it out?"

A nonverbal conversation ensued through the rearview mirror, where the man in the back glared at the driver. The young driver's shoulders scrunched up and his eyes snapped back toward the road.

She watched the man in the backseat. He wore a band on his left hand. She stared at his features, until he turned to look at her. She smiled. He ignored her and stared out the window.

She took in a deep breath, and lowered her voice, "So. *Joel*. Look, I know you think I'm the enemy, but Saul took his own life. I didn't kill him."

Joel turned toward her and stared like she was missing something big.

"I don't give a shit."

"Oh, okay. Good. So, you're a paid mercenary? Not one of the *family*, I take it?" He stared straight ahead, neither confirming nor denying. "Come on, I'm gonna die anyways, you might as well tell me."

He checked his watch again. "You talk too much."

"I do not," she huffed, crossing her arms. "And pardon me for trying to get my mind off the fact, they're gonna kill me when we get there." Kirin stared out the window. She needed to prepare her mind—what she'd just spoken was true.

After a long silence, he spoke. "Paid, yes. Not blood, but loyal."

She spun toward him and spat, "Loyal? To an organization that tortures and kills innocent people?" He stared at her, like she was lying. "Your parents alive?" She didn't wait for his answer. "Mine aren't. They killed my mother and enslaved my father. Maybe you knew him? Sonny Terhune?"

Joel shook his head. His eyes showed sincerity and she believed he didn't. Maybe he didn't know his employer as well as she thought. Or maybe he did. Just then, the phone in his pocket squawked. He dug it out and stared at the number before answering.

"Team one. No, sir. No casualties here. Yes, we have the package. No, no word from team two." Joel looked again at his watch. "Longer than planned. Pull extraction back ten minutes."

He hit the end button and glanced at the driver through the mirror. The driver nodded. Joel looked out the window and spoke, "The extraction point is gonna be tricky." Joel turned and looked her dead in the eyes.

"If you care at all about the people trying to save you, you'll come willingly. If not, they'll die."

Chapter Twenty-Two

Joel's brown eyes held a conflicted honesty. He'd been generous to prepare her for what might happen at the extraction point. Maybe he was easing his conscience or paying her back for caring for his wound. Either way, he wasn't what she expected.

Peach-fuzz driver made a sharp right turn, leading them on to a two-lane highway dotted with trailers and farms. The landscape was slightly different than her neck of the woods. But she felt like she'd seen this part of Tennessee before.

Joel's knee bounced nervously again. He cleared his throat, took off his seatbelt and scooted toward the front, glancing at her out of the corner of his eye. She strained but could only hear one side of their conversation.

"Stick close to me and don't try to be a hero. Get her in the boat. I'll hold 'em off."

Joel listened to what the young man had to say, then laughed. A nervous, but hearty, gut laugh poured out. The driver's eyes danced in the mirror as he too laughed. They had a bond like they were related but looked nothing alike. Joel sat back and re-buckled his belt.

These guys didn't seem like the enemy. They didn't seem like hard core mob types at all. This puzzled her. So, if they weren't in it for the family, then it was for the money. She was being drug in, so they could get rich. Her face felt flushed as she balled her fists.

"How much?" She spat.

Joel's demeanor flipped to defensive in an instant. "How much *what*?"

"How much did they pay you to deliver me?" His jaw tightened. When he didn't answer, she continued. "Did they tell you I'm a widow, with two little boys? That's who you're delivering to them. My only crime was being related to my father. And they'll make a sport of killing me, Joel. And my boys will be orphaned. They'll only have each other to lean on."

Joel turned his back on her silently stewing out the window. Kirin took a deep breath and changed tactics.

"Have you got brothers?"

Joel turned and stared at her now, like he was seeing her for the first time. "One."

"Then you know, it's a love/hate relationship, right?"

For the first time, the edges of his lips turned up. "True."

"Is he older or younger?"

"Older. Wiser. Bossier and prissier. Mine is a piece of work."

"Worse than you?" She asked, eyebrows up.

Joel nodded, "way worse than me." She couldn't help but notice the longing in his voice. She thought of Will and how Little Jack might describe him someday. She wondered what they'd be like when they grew up. What they'd become. Her only hope was that they'd be happy.

She wouldn't be there to see it.

Joel watched her and she cleared her throat. "I'll bet he's a picnic compared to you." She said, half joking.

He searched her eyes and agreed.

The car slowed. "Uh, Joel?"

Joel bolted upright, unhooked his belt and swore an oath under his breath. Kirin raised her body up to see a long stretch of road ahead, and traffic at a full stop in front of them. Like a jackrabbit on speed, Joel barked out directions while shoving two guns inside the black bag and slinging it on his back.

"See that patch of trees? Pull into the grass close to them, jump out and lift the hood. Turn your flashers on."

The truck slowed. Joel pushed Kirin's bad shoulder down, so her head wasn't visible. She winced, and he noticed. She reached down to re-tie one of her boots. The driver did what he was told and parked the truck right next to the trees. Joel grabbed hold of the young man's arm before he could open the door. "Watch your back." He cared about the boy, she could tell.

As soon as the young man opened his door and lifted the hood, Joel pushed Kirin's door open and shoved her out. With one hand on her back, he pushed her body to run crouched like they were boarding a helicopter.

When they hit the woods, they ran side by side for a long time until she signaled to him. She had to stop. Her lungs burned. Joel growled, glanced at his watch as Kirin bent over, hands on her knees to breathe.

Joel finally spoke. "We've got ten minutes to make it to the extraction point. It's a little over a mile. There will be gunfire, but I'll get you safely on the boat."

"*Safely?*" Still bent, she turned and looked at him like he had three heads. "That's like saying, I'll place you gently inside the lion's den right before dinner."

"Whatever." He waved her off. "I'll take you as far as the house, but after that I'm gone."

"*Whatever.* Good luck sleeping at night." She looked down at the gold band on his left hand. "Wonder what your wife will think of you. I bet you have little kids too, don't ya? They'll know. They always find out, you know."

Joel's face turned beet red. She'd hit a nerve.

"Move out."

Kirin took a deep breath and jogged alongside him. The kindness he'd shown her was finished. She was now only a paycheck to this man. This family man with a wife and kids. Then it dawned on her. What if they'd threatened his family? What wouldn't she do for hers? Would she turn someone over to them if they had Jack or Will? No…Well if she was being honest, maybe. She couldn't definitively answer that because she knew as a parent she'd do anything to keep them safe.

Even with the sun setting over the water, what should've been a beautiful sight, looked ominous and threatening. They ran until they could see the clearing up ahead, then slowed to a stop. She had to get her breathing under control if they were going to sneak up on whomever would be there.

She'd already made the decision to put her head down and run. But what if Sam was there? Couldn't she just run to him? She could, and he'd save her, but then how would she find Stacy? In her heart she knew her friend was back inside that horrible place and she couldn't live with herself if she didn't at least try to get her out. Plus, she still held onto the idea that she could stop these people. Although, she had no magic envelope this time.

When they'd crept to the clearing, a small open field lay before them that butted up to the lake. Beyond a patch of scraggly trees at the water's edge, was a small black boat. In the dying sun, it was hard to see anything except the rocking of the boat. It looked abandoned and unmanned. Kirin sat on a patch of pine straw and stretched her legs.

Joel sat a few feet away, glanced at his watch and took a long breath. "Delivering you, protects my family. I'm sorry about that. But there are people on the inside who'll help you."

Kirin stared at him for a beat before looking away. His face was sincere. This was why he didn't seem like them. He wasn't one of them, but someone pressed into service to protect his family. Probably ex-military and they needed his skill set. Kirin stood and brushed off her pants, not allowing him to see the mist in her eyes.

"Let's get to it, then." She readied herself to run into the open field.

Joel cinched up his pack and grabbed her hand. She pretended it was a kindness, but he probably didn't want her to trip or run toward those that might be there to save her.

Joel counted to three and they took off like a rocket. His long legs made him stride like a gazelle, while she seemed to be tiny stepping like a penguin. But in a flash, they were halfway to the boat. Both of their heads swung from side to side. She felt like she was running through an unmanned haunted house, just waiting for someone to jump out and yell, 'Boo!'

Nobody came to save her. Not a soul. Then she remembered. She was bait. They wouldn't stop her here because they were trying to find the hideout. A feeling of dread felt like a black cloud hanging over her, just waiting for the opportune moment to rain.

When they reached the other side, a wrinkled, fat man popped up from the driver's seat and pointed a rifle at Joel's head. Joel skidded to a stop.

"Team one, reporting."

The old man looked from him to Kirin and lowered his gun. "Hurry up, you're late. Where's two?"

Joel shrugged as he held out a hand to Kirin to help her aboard. She refused it and climbed onto the boat herself. He watched her. Although she didn't question his motives, she refused to make eye contact with him. He'd handed her over to die. She flopped onto a bench, just behind the driver.

The old man smelled like he'd licked a pack of Marlboro's. With hatred filling his eyes, he picked up a life jacket and chucked it at her head, hard. She caught it, glared at him, and put it on. This was how she'd expected to be treated.

Joel stood on the bank, shook his head then climbed in.

The stinky old man stared at him. "What the hell?"

"You need a lookout while you drive. You can take me back after. Team Two will be there by then."

"Suit yourself."

The old man threw the small boat into reverse, then took off down the lake at full speed. Damn, the cold air cut through her sweatshirt. She remembered it had a hood and pulled it on but had to hold it as the wind tried it's best to rip it from her head.

Joel sat across from her, on full alert. It was curious. She'd overheard a conversation at the barracks that they couldn't find The Club's local fortress anywhere.

Even though Stacy had lived there, she couldn't describe exactly where it was, only that it was a rehabbed mansion on the outside, but the inside was something out of a horror movie. A place where people were taken to the dungeon, tortured, and died. Kirin shuddered, which had nothing to do with the cold.

The sun was a half glowing orb that appeared to be sinking into the water. The boat slowed, but no house came into view. Only miles and miles of lake and trees. The old man's bald head turned toward Joel.

"Supplier's already there," he yelled over the noise.

Joel looked confused but seemed to recover quickly.

"Yeah? I didn't think they were supposed to arrive until tonight."

The man scoffed, "Asshole thinks he's better than us. More refined. Like his drugs are the best and we can't afford 'em. It's all bullshit. Nicky'll show 'em what a true family looks like." The man cut his eyes toward Kirin, then back to Joel. "He'll make a show of how we treat our enemies."

The old man hacked and coughed, lifting an old brown handkerchief to his lips, then shoving it into his back pocket. She was to be entertainment for their dinner guest. A show of power. Her legs began to tremble. She stretched them out to stop them from shaking. Escape plans ran through her mind. She was a good swimmer. But, unless she knocked both the dumbass driver and Joel out, they'd catch her. She could take the old man's rifle, which was propped up next to the wheel, but then could she shoot Joel? She felt like she'd connected with him.

An image of her boys danced across her mind. She swallowed the huge lump forming in her throat. This boat was taking her to her end. What would happen to them? She'd miss their whole lives. Graduations, proms, weddings and grandbabies—all seemed like fairytales now. She knew her aunt and uncle would raise them well, like they'd raised her. But damn it, she wanted to be there. Kirin swiped at her eyes. But if she didn't stop these killers now, they'd come after her boys.

No.

How had her life come to this? And what of Sam? If these people had their way, Sam would be with Gianna and Kirin would be dead. His life would be forever enslaved to those people, like it'd been since he was sixteen.

No.

Then there was Stacy. She knew her friend was there. *Felt it*. She couldn't leave her to save her own skin. They'd tortured Stacy because of Kirin. Tortured her to the point of almost mind twisting Stacy to believe she hated Kirin. Plus, she'd made Stacy a promise. She couldn't live with herself if she escaped without her.

No.

The lake curved around a corner, then straightened out. Just when the sun dipped below the trees and she thought they would have to navigate in the dark, they slowed and headed for a tree lined bank. Just beyond the trees, she saw a sprinkling of lights.

Even from a distance, it looked like a dilapidated dock she wouldn't allow her dog to walk on. Joel stood quick and looked around. Nobody was there to greet them or take Kirin off his hands. The old man butted the boat up to the dock. Joel huffed, grabbed his bag and motioned for Kirin to stand. When she did, he stripped her of the lifejacket and spun her around, handcuffing her once more. His hands were gentle, but his actions weren't.

Joel climbed onto the dock, then grabbed her by the elbow and helped her on to it as well. No sooner than her foot had left the boat, the gruff driver lit a cigarette and slammed the boat in reverse.

Joel navigated the uneven dock, helping her jump from it onto the eroded ground, still holding her up at the elbow. She noticed he'd switched sides and was holding her good elbow. Ahead lay a patch of trees. Joel threw his bag on his back then pulled her along as he jogged through the knobby, unkempt grass toward the trees. After a moment, he slowed, then stared straight ahead as he spoke.

"Once we reach the house, I'm gone. Keep your head about you. And remember not everybody inside is against you."

Kirin stared. Was he referring to the mole? Or maybe *he* was the mole? She'd love to think he wasn't entirely bad.

When they'd trotted to the edge of the small forest, she stopped. A looming, dark mansion rose up from the side of a hill looking like something out of a horror film. If there'd been spooky music or lightning, she'd have run the other way. The façade was made of moldy brick and old stone. It looked like a rundown, miniature Biltmore. It had to be at least a hundred years old. And some of the turrets and statues had crumbled to the point of being unrecognizable.

But even though it was spooky, there was something familiar about this place. She'd seen it before. She just knew it. In the paper or on the news…she wracked her brain. Finally it came to her. The local TV station, WBIR had run a piece on this place a few months back. It'd been left by a widow to the University of Tennessee in honor of her father, with strict stipulations that it was not to be sold but used by each incoming president of the college.

Her lungs stung with the cold air as they trudged on and her mind spun.

The widow's name was Eugenia Williams. Since the college presidents wanted to pick out their own homes, the house stood abandoned and vandalized for twenty years. The reporter had indicated that the University challenged the will and won, selling the property to an investor. The house was to be revamped and restored to its glory days.

As they moved closer, she noticed scaffolding attached to the brick in the back. The main structure was at least fifty yards long, and two stories. Balconies overlooked the lake from the top floor. Wrought iron finials and crumbling gargoyles adorned the roofline, making it look like a castle and showcasing it's early 1900's roots. Two fireplace stacks could be seen from the lake, but no smoke billowed out.

All shades were drawn. Very little happy light shone through. As they reached the house, Joel squeezed her arm. A grungy man dressed in a suit too big for his frame, stood quick and snuffed out his cigarette, pointing his gun, too late, at Joel.

Joel shook his head, "Team one."

The man lowered his gun, then looked Kirin up and down. "That her?"

Joel ignored his question, "Be on the lookout for team two."

The man licked his lips at her, then flopped back on the wrought iron chair to wait.

Joel ushered her inside and stopped. Her eyes adjusted. They'd entered a long parlor with several couches, but no people. He glanced about the room. Gripping her elbow tighter, he led her off to the left, through two small sitting rooms, toward a door that looked like a tiny, musty old closet.

When he opened it, it smelled like one too. Joel ushered her inside and followed. She felt like an elephant in a phone booth. In the back of the closet was a hidden door. Joel fidgeted with the rusty latch that looked exactly like the one on her farmhouse screen door. With a grunt, he opened the door. Rickety, splintered wooden stairs led down. Joel went first, sideways, still holding her elbow. The rungs were narrow, and she was grateful he held on to her tightly. More than once her foot slipped out from underneath her.

At the bottom, dark concrete hallways jetted out in three directions. Joel looked around, his eyes scrunched like he was trying to remember which way to go. He picked the hallway to the right and scurried along its path.

It was a cave of sorts. Cold, damp gray walls littered with only a sliver of light every ten feet. Under one of the lights, she glanced up at him. His face held determination and something else.

Fear.

In the distance, a faint cry echoed, stopping her in her tracks. She strained to hear. Joel stopped too. It appeared to be coming from every direction. The sound alone caused her blood to boil.

It was a cry she knew.

Chapter Twenty-Three

Rosa smiled in the rearview mirror as Will chattered the whole way to school. *Nonstop.* Not a nervous or anxious chatter, but more like an excited one. Competitive hallway paper football with his friends was all he breathed. And he was in the lead.

Dean and Kathy had made extra sure he hadn't heard any of their conversations with Sam.

Rosa had her own bodyguard of course, but she could move faster than that old coot. Besides, nothing was going to get to her baby. If there was one thing she learned on the street it was to be fierce and to notice everything. It's how she'd picked Kirin out of all the harried moms at the grocery store the day they'd "met."

Rosa's head swiveled back and forth at every light from Dean and Kathy's house to Will's school. She felt like she was driving a precious gem to market. One that everyone wanted to steal. A few times, she'd thought she was being followed, but she'd sped up to ensure she'd lost them. The only time he got wind of anything being different is when he questioned why she'd taken so many side streets. She'd chalked it up to being old.

When she pulled up to the school, she only recognized a few teachers opening the car doors for the kids. Sam had been taking Will to school more than she and Kirin had and it'd been a while since she'd dropped him off. The school's security officer was different, too. The big house of a man, Officer Greg, that never stopped talking was now replaced by a small dark headed man—no it was a woman. It was hard to tell from the back.

When Mrs. Whitney flung open Will's door, Rosa startled. *Damn happy morning people.*

"Hi Will! Good Morning, Rosa," she chirped.

Rosa exhaled, then touched Will on the arm. When he turned, he flashed her one of his best smiles. A smile that said she was his and he was hers. It always warmed her heart when her big kid did that. She hoped he'd do that all the way to high school.

As he flung on his backpack and walked toward the front doors, she answered Mrs. Whitney the same as she used to when he was smaller:

"Keep him safe."

Mrs. Whitney smiled, "Always!"

Rosa checked her mirrors and pulled out.

Now that Will was safe at school and Little Jack was safe at Kathy's, it was time for a quick meeting with her informant…without getting caught.

Chapter Twenty-Four

Kirin sprinted ahead blindly. Running toward the cry. Joel swore under his breath as she'd tore away from him and got the jump on him. His long legs caught up to her fast. The hallway was littered with closed doors. The first door she came to, she tried knocking it open with her body. It didn't work.

Joel grabbed her and spun her around to face him, whispering through gritted teeth. "Damnit Lane be quiet. What are you doing?"

Kirin twisted, showing him her hands, "Take them off—please. I swear, I won't run from you. Please Joel."

Joel's expression was that of a man who wanted nothing further to do with this place. He blew out a long breath, then lifted the tail of his black jacket and pulled keys off the carabiner attached to his pants. He flipped through quick and agile and found the key. Pulling it off his key ring, he turned her the rest of the way around and unlocked the cuffs. Without a word, he stuffed the key into her back pocket.

Kirin didn't hesitate. She begged, "Help me find her."

Joel grabbed her by the arm. "I have to deliver you in the next three minutes or I'm dead."

"She's down here…My friend Stacy. Put me in a cell with her. Tell them…tell them I was a freakin' nightmare and you needed to secure me somewhere before finding them."

Joel's long legs began to move and without the cuffs, Kirin could move just as fast. They sprinted together from door to door, listening. The cry stopped, damnit. Kirin let out a low whistle. Joel stared at her wide-eyed then slid her a look that said, "you're going to get us killed."

Two doors down from where they stood, she heard a tiny voice, "I'm here."

Kirin ran to the door and shook the handle. No dice. Joel strode up and felt along the wall. An oval shaped button, camouflaged by being the same drab grey as the walls, had been placed next to the door. Joel pressed his right thumb against the oval until the door clicked. Kirin opened it wide and gasped.

The room was four walls of stone and small like a good sized walk-in closet. When they opened the door, Stacy looked like a work of art. Wearing only a pink bra and matching panties, Stacy stood frozen, holding a hard backed chair over her head, ready to clobber the next person who walked in. Her body quaked, and her eyes were wide with fear. Stacy's body was covered in bruises. Kirin held both hands up and took in the sad sight of her friend. Stacy's pretty face was splattered with dark red blood.

When she saw Kirin, she dropped the chair and ran to her, holding her like her life depended on it. The only sound in the room was the chattering of Stacy's teeth.

"I'm...so...so sorry," Stacy rambled, sobbing. "Why are you here? I'm so glad to see you." Her body trembled. Joel stripped out of his jacket and handed it to Kirin. It was then, Stacy's head snapped up and she noticed him.

"*You!*" she spat. Stacy took a step toward him putting Kirin between them. Stacy's voice quivered with anger reverberating through every syllable. "*You* brought her here?"

"You two know each other?" Kirin wrapped the jacket around her friend. Then, without thinking, raised her hands up between them like she was a boxing referee.

"Yeah. This scum was supposed to be on our side, but the turncoat went for the money. He's a hired thug—only in it for himself." Then she spoke over Kirin's head at Joel, "You know they have you by the balls now, right? They own you. If I were you, I'd divorce your pretty wife and hide your cute little kids, because nothing will stop them." Stacy's voice softened at the end. She staggered a little then sat on the hard-backed chair and winced.

Joel's face held nothing but anger. Red and blotched like he wanted to spit nails. He glanced at his watch. "I gotta go."

"Yes. Leave. You're good at that," Stacy hissed. They glared at each other like two dogs about to attack. Her next question hit Kirin like a truck. "Wait, we need his gun."

"Shut up, Stace." Kirin began to pace. "We're not entertaining that. We'll figure a way out of here."

"How?" Stacy cried. "Do you have any idea who they have up there? Some freakin' drug lord from the Detroit cartel. They're making some deal tonight. That man makes Nicky look like a Sunday School teacher." Stacy stood and began to pace, not even caring that she was mostly naked. "And not only that, but our guys aren't gonna be able to find us. There were no trackers and they've been searching for this place for months."

Kirin felt a pang of fear watching Joel head for the door. She touched his shirt and he turned.

Before she could say anything, he spoke. "You said if I let you out of the cuffs, you wouldn't run. You gotta trust me. And stay down here."

Joel turned, opened the door, and closed it behind him. When the door clicked, Kirin felt an overwhelming sense of sadness. She'd bonded with him. She turned back to see her friend, staring at the opposite wall. Her expression said she'd already given up. Already decided it was no use.

Stacy let out a defeated breath, stood and rubbed her forehead. Pointing at Kirin's feet she said, "Nice work boots, where'd ya get those dinosaurs?"

Kirin lifted one boot, "The closet in our room, back at the airstrip."

Stacy leaned over, "What's that silver thing on the bottom?"

Kirin sat on the wooden chair, yanked her boot off and turned it over. A tiny silver circle was wedged between the treads of the boot. Kirin pulled it off and inspected it. Stacy snatched it out of her hand and turned it over.

"It's gotta be a transmitter," Stacy's smile crept across her face as she handed it back. "Of course. The Club would come after you and your shoes would lead the FBI straight to the mob. Did you know you were gonna be bait?"

She'd known but hadn't even thought to look at her shoes. Kirin nodded and shoved the circle in her pocket as a plan hatched in her mind.

"Listen. Is there any way out of this room other than the door?"

Stacy shrugged then glanced up at an access panel in the ceiling. Perfect, except it took a screwdriver to release the square grate. Kirin took the chair and placed it under the air return. Standing on the chair, she was barely tall enough to reach it. But Stacy was taller. Stacy shook her head and switched places.

A single gunshot echoed in the hallway. Close. Remarkably close. Both women froze. A man's voice yelled something Kirin couldn't understand. They needed to hurry. Kirin pulled the circle from her pocket and handed it to Stacy. Stacy's hand trembled as she used the edge to loosen the screws.

Two screws down. Stacy's fingers furiously twisted the third screw as another shot rang out. Even closer. This time a man screamed out in pain. Kirin climbed up on the chair with Stacy, grabbed the circle and worked on the 4th screw, whispering as she did.

"Listen. I'm gonna disappear *temporarily*."

Stacy's fingers froze. Her head snapped toward Kirin.

Kirin locked eyes with her, "I'm not leaving you. Do you understand me? But if they catch me here, we're both dead."

Stacy nodded. Tears formed in her eyes. The third and fourth screws came off together, causing the grate to give way. The women caught it, but the wooden chair creaked and wobbled, causing a loud scraping sound. They both froze.

When nothing happened outside the door, Stacy took the grate, stepped off the chair and propped it up against a wall.

Climbing back up she made a pocket as Kirin had done earlier and hoisted her friend inside the hole.

Once inside, Kirin's eyes adjusted. Her body was hunched over in the tight space as darkness engulfed her. Warm air whooshed past. She had to be inside the heat and air duct. But instead of using silver flexible ductwork, this old house had a two by two square plywood tunnel that snaked around between floors. Her heart pounded, reminding her she wasn't a fan of small spaces.

Had she been five pounds heavier, like she was before the blast, there'd be no way she would've fit. As it was, she was having a hard time turning her body back around to face Stacy. She felt like a German Shepard in a kitten cage. Turning her head and squeezing her shoulder through, she finally faced the way she'd come. The plywood underneath her creaked.

She was determined to give Stacy hope and confidence. Kirin took a deep breath then peered back at Stacy who with a resolute look on her face, took off Joel's jacket and handed it up through the hole. Kirin grabbed it and tied it securely around her waist. Then, reached back down and handed Stacy the silver circle. It'd help her brother and the rest of the FBI to find her.

"I'll be back for that."

"Damn well better," Stacy said. Strength emanated from her voice, but her body shook. Stacy and Kirin held hands and locked watery eyes before Kirin turned back to crawl into darkness.

God, she hated leaving her friend to battle whoever came through the door. But this was the right thing to do, she just knew it.

Kirin grunted as she wedged her shoulders against the wood and turned back toward the tunnel. Rough plywood skimmed Kirin's shoulders and the heat blowing in her face made sweat appear at her temples. The tiny bit of light disappeared as Stacy replaced the grate. When the heat suddenly stopped, the only sound in the tunnel was the squeak of each of the screws as Stacy turned them.

She prayed she was right.

Chapter Twenty-Five

Kirin's ears perked up. Scampering of tiny feet told her the resident rodents knew she was there even if the mob didn't. With each placement of her hand, crumbles of dirt and God-knows-what-else stuck to her palms. She shuddered. Careful, she put each hand down then placed her weight on it. Since the house on top of her was built in the forties, who knew when the dungeon and air system were added.

The last thing she wanted to do was to make an unwelcome entrance into a lower room by falling through rotted wood or push up through a floor grate right into a hornet's nest.

As she slow-crawled, Sam's handsome face crossed her mind. She prayed he hadn't been captured. Her stomach lurched. *Gianna.* The snake was surely somewhere above, waiting for her to break her beloved's heart so she could pick up the pieces. Maybe there was a way to fix this without handing over the love of her life.

A flood of striped light shone down into the pipe just ahead. Low, muffled voices floated to her ears. Kirin stilled. If she moved a few more feet, she'd be able to pick up words. Careful not to make a sound, she pressed on slowly and stopped in the darkness, just before the rectangle of light.

Just then, the heat inside the pipe kicked back on. Warm air blew past her and up the grate. It was loud like she was in a wind tunnel. She closed her eyes and craned her neck to get closer. The voices were muffled, but she could make out most of the words.

"You're sure the cash is all there?" The click-clack of heels and a voice she now knew better than her own was loud and clear. *Gianna.* But her tone didn't have that confident edge it had before. She almost sounded nervous.

"Yes, counted and hidden. Now let's hope nobody fucks this up," Nicky's gravelly voice rang out directly above her. "Even though they hijacked our last two shipments of girls—and I swear to God when I find out who our informant is, I'm gonna kill them—we got back part of our powder the government stole from us." All light in the pipe ceased as he crouched down and held his palms over the grate. Kirin stilled and held her breath. "Why is this house so damn cold?"

"Where's pin-head?" Gianna asked, clearly ignoring his question.

"Todd headed out back to smoke. Took Geno with him."

"If he screws this up…" Gianna's voice was tight and held a warning.

"If he does, we're done with him. It won't matter that he's family."

"I'm done no matter what, *Nicola*. Sam and I head back to Cleveland tonight."

Kirin balled her fists. Her jaw ached. Damn overconfident woman—counting her chickens before they're hatched. Or men in this case.

Nicky lowered his voice, "It's father, or dad or anything but *Nicola*. And you can't. The Club needs you. We agreed, Todd can't lead. And there's nobody better to take this over. Sauly spent all the money he had left on this piece-of-shit house for mama. You and I can build this empire back to what it was before Sauly was murdered and the fucking government took the rest of his money."

Nicky shuffled away and cleared his throat. "Look, I don't trust the fucker, but if you love him, Sam can stay. I won't kill him, I swear. But that bitch he's with has to die."

Gianna clomped across the hardwood, "How many times? How many times I gotta say it? I don't want this! Never have. I'm an attorney for Christ's sake! You pushed your only child into being a *whore*. I'm out. And I swear to God, you try to force my hand old man, I'll end you."

The door opened. Another set of feet crossed the wood floor. It groaned and creaked under the weight. Nicky moved away from the vent. Kirin felt her body relax a tiny bit.

Gianna spoke, "Well? Is he here?"

A faint male voice said, "Team two hasn't made it yet."

"Then it's your job. Go get him. Bring him here." Gianna whined like a child begging for a toy.

"You know I can't do that," the male voice coming from the corner, said.

"You listen to me. I don't care what your relationship is like—I paid you handsomely out of *my* money to do a job. You will bring him to me."

Nicky interrupted, "Just got word. Team two is here, battered, but they're here."

The click clack of quick steps running across the wood floors meant Gianna trotted out of the room. Jealous tingles crept up Kirin's body. The only good thing was Sam was alive, but he was inside the lion's den, too.

"Everything is set," Nicky said when the door slammed.

"What now?" The man's voice had a familiar ring to it but strained. *Joel.*

"Go get her. I want her naked and bound. Make sure she's tied up tight and bring her to the main foyer."

"Yes, sir."

~*~

Kirin crawled faster. Her arms shook. He was either talking about her or Stacy. Either way, she didn't have time to think, just move. When the whooshing air cut off, she had to slow. The plywood creaked with her weight and she had no idea if the rooms above or below could hear it.

The labyrinth of connecting passageways seem to spider off in all directions. Underneath this decrepit house was a small city. Hell, she could be so turned around, she might not even be heading toward the main foyer. Every few feet, she'd stop and listen. Echoes of conversations rattled through the canal and each time, she'd follow the path. She twisted, turned and crawled, and only one time had to reverse.

The air seemed warmer and stuffier at the same time. She must be getting closer to the unit. Her hope was that the unit was closest to the main part of the house.

At one turn, she heard music and stopped. Eminem. Swear to God, the room above played *Eminem*—old Eminem at that. She stilled, on all fours and automatically mouthed the words to "Soldier." Whoever was above was probably about her age. She crawled until light from a square grate appeared, then stopped to listen.

A door opened, then closed and the music stopped.

"What up?" A deep male voice rang out in the silence.

"Why the fuck are we still waiting?" a different gruff voice asked.

The first voice, now farther away answered, "almost time."

"All's I gotta say is they better have the money or Leo's gonna go on a rampage."

"I just overheard one of the hillbillies say they heard our stuff is chemical bullshit."

Silence.

An angry gunshot rang out so loud she had to slap her hand across her mouth to muffle her scream. The hole in the wood just two feet ahead of her, smoked. If she'd crawled farther, she'd be dead.

"We'll show them chemical bullshit. Let's move."

The door slammed shut.

It took a full minute for Kirin to get her breathing under control and her ears to stop ringing. When her heart rate slowed, she crawled several more feet until she came to another juncture in the wooden tunnel. To the right, the space seemed lighter. It'd make more sense to find a dark room and see if she could jimmy her body up through a grate.

Heading to the left, the heat kicked back on. A whistle up ahead told her the air was squeezing through an opening. She crawled another ten feet until the light changed. It looked more like moonlight shone through a window into a dark room above her. It illuminated the grate just enough for her to see the outline of the tunnel.

She waited, listening for sounds of sleepy breathing. No noise. It seemed nobody occupied the room above her. Underneath it now, she squinted to look through the slats in the grate. Something fuzzy covered part of the grate. She stuck her pinky through. It was soft, like a blanket.

She hoped there wasn't a sleeping baby or something in this room. She could only make out large shadows. Furniture maybe? Maybe a large bed, a dresser, and a couch.

Kirin positioned her body directly underneath. Her plan was to push her good shoulder into the grate, moving it slightly with a prayer it didn't squeak. When she situated her hands under her, one landed on something hard. Kirin recoiled in the dark.

She reached back out and felt it. Paper. A rectangle of wrapped paper, like a present. With one hand holding her up, the other flipped it over. It landed back on the plywood with a thud. Whatever it was, it was heavy, not as hard as a brick, but pliable. She moved her fingers around each end, then it hit her.

Cash. It was a stack of wrapped cash. She lowered one elbow to the floor and used her other hand to untie Joel's jacket from her waist. Fumbling around in the dark, she located the zipper and found an inside phone pocket the perfect size to secure the brick of cash. Shoving it in and retying the jacket, she hunched over, cross-legged and used one shoulder to push the grate.

It was slow going. The grate made a rubbing sound but didn't squeak like she'd feared. As soon as the lip cleared the edge of the hardwood floor, she lifted it with both hands and placed it on the blanket. Popping her head through the square, she feared if someone were inside, they'd see her. She must've looked like a whack-a-mole.

When the heat kicked off, the room was eerily quiet. Kirin hoisted herself into the room and crouched. The grate was under the window, with the bed between her and the door. Her vision sharpened in the dark. She crouched completely still and searched all corners for movement. Nobody there, thank God. She crawled a foot toward the window seat then shook her head. *Stand up, ding dong.* She stood cautiously, then stretched.

Ten-foot ceilings with ornate crown-molding made her feel especially small in the giant room. Peering out the window to get her bearings, she cupped her hands against the glass. Shadows fell through the trees that lined the extensive driveway, looking like a line of soldiers protecting the house.

She made it to the front. She'd crawled from the basement through tunnels and made it where she wanted to go, even with her wonky sense of direction. Holy crap. She smiled in the dark.

The doorknob rattled. Kirin slapped a hand across her mouth to stop an escaping scream. Not enough time to replace the grate. She scurried under the bed. The door swung open and the lights flicked on.

Chapter Twenty-Six

Large black boots stomped into the room. Their owner paused just inside the door. She blinked rapidly, eyes watering from the bright light.

"What the…?" The deep male voice swore an oath then ran around the bed to the grate lying next to the hole. When the man dropped to his knees, he laid his face on the hardwood and shoved one arm inside. She held her breath. If he'd turned his head toward the door instead of the window, he'd have looked her in the eye.

Rising to his knees, he dug in his pocket, pulled out his phone and turned on the flashlight. Diving headfirst, he was inside the hole up to his waist.

Now. Sneak out the open door. *Move Kirin.* She stretched one leg toward the door and pulled her body slow and quiet toward it. Faster than she thought possible, the man stashed his phone and stood. He must've heard her. When the click of the safety rang out, she was sure he'd find her.

The man stood stock still. Her body trembled. Her quiet, shallow breaths made her lightheaded.

She'd always hated hide-and-seek for this very reason. She never could hide well and the anxiety of being found always made her nauseous. His boots made a slow thudding sound as he stalked around the bed toward the door, like he circled his prey.

At the last second, he changed trajectory. He walked toward the door, flicked off the light and turned toward the bed. From this angle she could see him from the neck down. When he spoke, his voice was a low whisper.

"You got about one minute to get out of this room, before it's crawling with them. I'll walk slow."

Wait…What? *Brandon*? Couldn't be…but, it was! He was alive! She'd never been so happy to hear Babyface's voice in all her life. As soon as the door clicked closed, she moved—quieter than she'd ever moved before. Kirin touched the inside pocket. Cash was still there. Now, time to get out of this room.

She crept to the door and turned the handle, slow and without noise. Opening it an inch, she peered out from the dark room into a dimly lit hallway.

Nothing. No noise, no people. She cracked it another inch, held her breath and ran to the left. The view from the window made her think she was on the right side of the house. She assumed the great room would be toward the center of the house. This was like being in one of those backyard hedge mazes. One wrong turn and she'd be sunk. She had to find it though, to intercept them with Stacy. How the hell she'd fight unarmed, she had no idea.

As she padded lightly down the hallway, she focused on finding the front door—only not to leave. But to find the great room. God if she only had a plan. Instead, she had zero idea what to do once she got there. If she could talk with the other cartel and somehow explain how barbaric these people were. Who was she kidding? Both sides were just as barbaric. She needed to dangle the money in front of the others and get herself, Brandon, Stacy and Sam out of that house. And Joel. Possibly him too.

Voices. Two deep voices bounced down the hall, around the corner. Kirin darted on her toes away from them, down the hallway frantically searching for a way out. A dark alcove with a door came into view just ahead.

She sprinted like her life depended on it.

Chapter Twenty-Seven

When Sam Neal's luck went wrong, it went way wrong.

Not only was he sporting a busted lip from his beautiful fiancé kicking him the night before, but now he had a matching black eye from allowing himself to be captured.

He'd watched them force Kirin into a van. His world had stopped. In the back of his mind, he'd known they'd come after her, but he'd thought he'd be right there to defend her. But he wasn't. He'd been too far away to stop it. And if they took her, there was no way to track her. They'd kill her for sport, and he knew it.

For once, his heart and his mind worked together.

Thinking at warp speed he surrendered to the nearest pimply faced idiot he could, but not before some steroid-filled jack-tard clocked him.

Bastard.

But that wasn't even the worst of it. He'd been brought in and dropped at Gianna's feet. Which, in truth, wasn't entirely horrible. They'd played cat and mouse with each other since they were teenagers. Then again, he never knew which side Gianna was on.

Most of the time, she was on the side of herself.

But now…now, he stood toe to toe with the only person he hadn't expected to see inside the enemy's lair.

Seth.

His baby brother had just entered the room and stood a foot in front of him. He was an inch taller with more hair than Sam. The moment he walked in, the room's energy changed. It always did. Even when they were competing as kids. But that was all on him, not Seth. Seth had looked up to him, wanted to emulate his every move and Sam would have nothing of it.

He'd protected the little—now big—shit his whole life. Protected him from the snares of The Club, forbidding him to even meet the same people Sam and his father knew.

Despite that, here he stood in the middle of a parlor of this old crumbling mansion, working for the damn enemy. And not only that but smirking like he had some sort of secret.

All Sam's protective maneuvers shot to shit.

Seth glared at his brother for a beat and then without acknowledging Sam, he spoke over the top of his head to Gianna, "Geno's bringing the prisoners up now. The Detroit boys caught me in the hall. They're tired of waiting. I showed them to the formal living room."

His voice had deepened even more. When did that happen? Hell, he was twenty-nine, so it happened a long time ago. But it still sounded weird. Seth had been born shortly before Sam was "recruited." A baby late in life, his mama had said. Sam wasn't around much, but he loved his brother enough to know Seth didn't need any part of this corruption in his life.

When Seth finished talking, Gianna nodded. She had a damn cat-like grin painted on too.

Obviously, she knew who he was.

"Sam," Joel stated as a greeting like they were old gunslinging enemies.

"What are you doing here?" Fists balled, Sam's angry voice shook more than he'd wanted it to.

"Working. You?" There was a twinkle in Seth's eye, even as his jaw muscles flexed and tightened.

"You're a damn fool. You have no idea who you're working for."

Seth agreed.

Gianna stalked over and snaked her arm through Sam's, "Oh, I think he knows."

Sam's mind churned. What did Gianna get out of bringing his baby brother here? She'd mentioned a replacement for him inside The Club, so that they'd let him out. Let them live happily ever after in Ohio. Like that would happen. But surely, she didn't mean his own brother.

And how in the hell was he gonna save his brother and Kirin and God-only-knew-who-else that got captured? He had to focus. Todd would be coming in any second and that man wanted him dead more than most.

When Todd and one of his cronies finally showed up through a side door, Todd eyeballed Sam. The hate there had been mutual for years. Gianna stalked toward Todd and lit into him immediately.

They weren't very deep into their bickering when the handle on the hallway door, just a foot away from Sam and Seth, jiggled. Both brothers spun in unison, drawing their weapons, and pointing them at the door.

That's when Sam realized his bad luck had only begun.

~*~

It didn't take a genius to know—she'd picked the worst possible door.

But when she'd opened it, tiptoed in, and closed it quietly behind her, she heard a click right next to her ear.

As she turned, five pairs of eyes and one gun stared her in the face.

The room itself was stuck in 1982 with mauve carpet, paisley bordered walls that almost looked pink. No furniture, except a table, couch, and a few random chairs.

Todd and Gianna stood on one side of the room, toe to toe, and obviously in the middle of a heated discussion.

The gun, safety off and shoved in her temple, was held by Sam.

Joel stood next to Sam and upon seeing her, holstered his gun.

The look on Sam's face was sheer murder. Her heart lurched at seeing him. Sam grabbed her good arm, holstered his gun, and spun her around roughly to face Gianna and Todd.

"See?" Gianna screeched at Todd, "I *told* you! He's finished with her."

The witch wore tailored cream pants, and a matching mid-waist jacket covering a low cut tank and heels. She looked like she belonged in a boardroom, not this old house.

Todd stared at Kirin like she was an alien. "Who let you out?"

Before she could answer, Gianna pulled Todd to the other side of the room, with her back to Kirin, Sam, and Joel. Her hands were on her hips as she spoke low to him. She looked like a mom lecturing her son. Kirin strained to hear their conversation but could only hear bits and pieces. She was certain she heard the word 'money.'

They must know by now it was taken. She'd set this ball into motion. Now, she just prayed it worked.

Joel slipped an arm through hers and tugged her toward him. When she glanced up, his eyes were trained on Sam, who glared right back over her head. The nonverbal fight going on between these two men was loud. She felt like a steak in the lion's den.

Joel stood slightly taller than Sam, and his attitude was written all over his face. Kirin was his prisoner, not Sam's. But Sam wasn't letting go. His body language was possessive, tight, and angry. Kirin took a long breath and tried to help.

"Joel, this is Sam. Sam, this is—"

Sam interrupted, "Seth, I need the truth. What the hell are you doing here?" Sam whispered quickly.

Seth?

"I don't go by that name anymore and you know it. I'm a grown man. And I don't have to run anything past you. You're not responsible for me."

Kirin interrupted, "Wait…I thought your name was Joel?"

Joel glanced down at her, "It is."

Sam was like a dog with a bone, he was not letting it go. "What does Jen think of you running with the mob?"

Joel fired back, "I wasn't running with *your mob*. I was hired by someone else to do a different job."

Sam looked perplexed. He pointed toward Gianna, "Did she know that we're brothers?"

Joel smiled, "Not at first. I think she does now, though."

Both men glanced over to ensure Gianna was still occupied by Todd. Kirin peered up from Sam to Joel. Yup. Same nose. She wondered why she hadn't seen it before.

"Gianna knew," Sam said more to himself than to anyone.

"Gianna guessed, but it was never confirmed. How about 'thank you' to your little brother for bringing your fiancé in without harm? And speaking of which, how did an asshat like you land somebody like her?" Kirin grinned automatically.

"Wait. Back up...other than Gianna, who hired you?"

Joel only shook his head, which made Sam's face turn beet red.

When Joel tried to pull Kirin toward him, Sam growled. Instinctively, she put her hands up like a ref stuck in between two hot headed boxers. The harsh, angry whisper from Sam made her eyebrows lift. "Let. Go."

Joel's teeth gritted, "Stay out of it, Sam."

Todd stepped around Gianna and stomped toward them. His eyes darted from one man to the other, his voice too high. "You're brothers?" then to Gianna, "And, of course you knew this, right?"

Gianna waved her arms. "No harm using someone who's already trained. And they don't speak to each other, so it works perfectly."

Sam looked like he could spit nails.

Todd scrubbed his face, "Does Nicky know this?"

Gianna just smiled.

Joel's eyes never wavered from Sam. Gently he pulled Kirin from his brother and led her by her bad arm toward a chair in the middle of the room. She watched both men. Unspoken words flying between them.

Joel locked eyes with Kirin. The tips of his lips turned up kindly when he motioned for her to turn. With a gentle touch he peeled his jacket from her waist and pulled it on. He placed a warm hand on her shoulder to sit and left it there.

Kirin's plan began to formulate, but for it to work, she needed to have one hundred percent faith that Joel would be

164

on her side. She glanced up at him. His jaw tight, he tore his gaze from his brother and nodded down at her.

The block of money inside Joel's pocket had to be drawing his jacket down on one side. There was no way he didn't feel it when he pulled it on. She prayed he wouldn't give back the only bargaining chip she had up her sleeve.

Sam's eyes locked with hers, then with his brother.

She'd seen that look—hell, she'd swam in it lately—jealousy.

Gianna must've seen it too. "Joel, search her, *now*."

Joel zipped his jacket then took Kirin by the elbow. His eyes held an apology as he raked his hands up and down her body, then her legs. Sam's body, just a few feet away, was rigid. She could've sworn she heard him growl.

Todd began to pace, then stopped and turned to Gianna. "Now what? If she doesn't have the fucking money, who does? G, they'll kill one of us if we've brought them here and the money is gone. This pact *must* work. Period. It's the only way to get back in business. They used a ton of operating cash to buy this hunk of shit house for Grandma. You know as well as I do that the business is broke."

Gianna stood for a beat. A sick smile played on her lips. She glanced at her expensive watch, then to Kirin.

"It's time. Time for the *entertainment* to start."

Chapter Twenty-Eight

Todd wrung his hands and picked up his suit jacket. He pulled out a pistol and shoved it down the back of his pants. Then let out a deep breath as he shrugged it on.

Sam pulled on a jacket over his stashed gun. When Gianna walked toward him with an outstretched hand, he refused to look at Kirin. He smiled warmly and took her hand. Then as their bodies were close enough to touch, he did something so personal that Kirin had to choke back a sob.

He pulled her in and kissed her on the forehead.

Joel had to lift Kirin out of the chair and lead her toward the door. Her legs wouldn't move.

Sam turned, with Gianna's hand in his and led the way out of the room and down the long hallway.

The pain in Kirin's chest felt like someone had shoved a hot knife in her heart. It stung deep. Especially when Gianna intertwined her fingers with his and kissed him on the cheek.

A forehead kiss in Sam's world meant love. He'd been forced too many times to show physical affection to get whatever The Club wanted, but Kirin knew those forehead kisses were genuine and real. Her eyes filled with tears. He loved Gianna.

But maybe it was just their shared past. Or maybe it was more. She'd like to think that he'd done it out of a sense of pity. But what if he'd finally answered her texts about sleeping together?

Kirin closed her eyes for a second. Tears streamed down her face and she let them fall. She tried not to watch them but couldn't seem to tear her eyes away.

Walking next to her and holding her by the arm, Joel cleared his throat. She cut her eyes up at him as Joel narrowed his. He shook his head as if to say *stop watching*.

Damn, she wished she could.

The only good thing…if Sam was pretending he was done with her, she wouldn't need to use Steve to break up with him. If Steve was even still alive.

As they came closer toward an open arched doorway, Nicky announced Todd's entrance and that the meeting was about to start.

Crossing the threshold into the room, Kirin took a quick look around.

Two hefty men dressed in black sat on the couch. One held a bloody towel covering most of his face, while the other had an eye that was so swollen, he needed an eye patch to cover his permanent blink.

Must be team two.

Just beyond them a figure was tied to a chair. She gasped. Wearing only her underwear, but now with one bra-strap snapped, was Stacy. Her make-up smudged under puffy eyes like she'd been crying. Her hair was all a mess with a look of sheer brokenness on her face.

Kirin let out a scream and came unglued on Joel— shoving, kicking and clawing to get to her friend. When Nicky, clearly embarrassed, cleared his throat, Joel reached out and grabbed her around the waist, lifting her off the floor.

"Stop. *Stop*." He ordered in her ear.

Kirin stilled. More thick tears ran down her face. Stacy glanced over at the commotion with a blank, detached look in her eyes. Kirin wasn't even sure her friend knew she was there.

They'd shattered her.

Nicky pointed to a chair with rope tied to it and plastic underneath. It was then, she noticed Stacy's chair had plastic underneath as well. They were both set to die in this room.

Joel carried her to the chair and sat her down, then pulled her arms behind her and tied them to the chair.

After a beat Todd cleared his throat, "Gentlemen, we have business to discuss, but first these two women have been a thorn in our side. They're not family. Both are traitors as far as we're concerned and need to be terminated."

Kirin followed Todd's line of sight to see three men standing on the opposite side of the great room. Two body-building thugs, each the size of a commercial double-door fridge flanked a flamboyant thin man with dark slanted eyes and perfectly manicured eyebrows. He wore a long white fur coat, black pants and women's boots. His short fingernails were painted black as well.

The look on Mr. Fur-lined's face was that of boredom. The two fridge-men, both with their chins high and wearing sunglasses, looked as if they could take out the whole room in their sleep. The barrel of an AR hung down the back of one of the men's legs.

Nicky's eyes, filled with hate, never moved from Kirin's face. His greasy smile unfolded when Todd announced, "Bring 'em in."

Nothing could've prepared Kirin for what she saw. The short-haired woman, who she saved in the airplane hangar walked into the room holding the arm of a blindfolded boy.

She knew instantly.

Her boy.

When the woman ripped the blindfold off him, he blinked and blinked. His eyes were swollen like he'd been crying.

"*No...*" Kirin's voice was tiny.

Sam took a step toward Will, but Gianna yanked him back.

"Mom?" Will's voice shook as their eyes locked. She could barely see him through her tears. *God no. Please no.* Joel's grip on her shoulder tightened. Kirin mouthed to Will— "stay still. It's gonna be okay. I love you."

Frantic she glanced at Sam. But Gianna's watery eyes and horrified look on her face told Kirin instantly, this wasn't Gianna's idea, nor did she know about it. Nobody was that good of an actress. Sam was beet red with fists balled down at his sides. At one point, he mouthed something to Will too, but she couldn't tell what.

Kirin locked on to the woman holding Will. If the daggers from her eyes could have killed the woman she'd be dead. She'd saved that bitch. Saved her from breathing her last breath inside that hangar. And she now held Kirin's child by the elbow.

The woman stared back at Kirin's glare, completely blank.

Kirin quick-judged the distance. She could be up, across the room, punch the woman in the face and grab Will before anyone caught her. They'd probably shoot her, but she didn't care. She scooted to the front of the chair and shifted her weight to the balls of her feet. Joel pushed down harder on her shoulder.

Three...two...

"Calamia." The man in the white fur coat stepped forward. His thick accent, she couldn't place, but his voice rumbled low and deep. Nicky and Todd turned.

"I don't give a shit about your family drama. I want my money. Now."

Nicky deflated and stared at the man as if to say, *'Now?'*

The man leveled a look at Todd as the two thugs walked around the man in the fur coat and one pulled out an AR and cradled it like a baby.

Nicky's head snapped toward Todd.

Todd was as white as the man's coat. He didn't have the money. She did.

Well, Joel did, now. This was her bargaining chip. She could use the money to save Will.

Todd inhaled sharply, threw his shoulders back and cleared his throat. "The money will be wire transferred when the banks open—"

"*That* was not our agreement," The man in the white coat crossed his arms.

Todd stuttered, "It was a bank mistake. The money was supposed to be ready and..."

The gunshot rang out then silenced the room. The hole in the wall next to Todd's head had a small ring of smoke that hung for a beat, then disappeared. Todd's eyes opened wide.

Fur coat man grinned, then nodded to the house-of-a-man to his right, who was still holding his pistol. Without a word the man sidestepped around him and casually walked toward Todd and Nicky.

When he reached them, he looked each one in the face and spoke low and eloquent. "Leo isn't fond of families that make promises and don't keep them. Our agreement was two hundred thousand cash. You have one minute to produce it, or one of you dies."

Nicky's face turned red and fighting mad.

The large man turned to walk back, when another close-range shot rang out.

This one was followed by a sickening thud of a body falling to the floor.

Chapter Twenty-Nine

Nicky stepped over Todd's crumpled body.

It heaped unnaturally on the floor like a bag of trash. He pointed the gun still in his hand at Gianna and motioned for her to join him in the middle of the room. Sam's body twitched.

Gianna's face held nothing but sheer hatred as she strutted across the floor toward her father.

Nicky turned back. Leo's AR toting muscle man had instantly aimed the rifle toward his forehead. Nicky waved him off like a gnat.

"No need." Then to Leo, "As you can see our family dynamics have changed. I apologize for my nephew's inadequate behavior. You'll have the money before you head back to Detroit. My daughter, Gianna, is an attorney and the new head of our family. She has political connections, street smarts and let's just say a very feminine way of getting what we want."

When Leo's gaze raked Gianna up and down and then he licked his lips, Nicky added, "And she's easy on the eyes, too."

Gianna's fists balled. Her stare turned cold.

Leo grinned, "I'm sure we can work something out."

Nicky turned toward Kirin, but spoke to Leo, "Give me two minutes."

He sauntered over to her, smiling like it was Christmas morning. Joel's body tensed.

Kirin had seen enough. And her boy had seen enough. Nicky was not going to murder her in front of Will. When he was only a few feet away, he stopped and stared. Joel's grip tightened on her shoulder.

Nicky drew his pistol and aimed it at her head, then spoke low, "You will die today. And don't worry about your boy…Gianna will raise him to be one of us. I own him. He'll be the slave I never had. And I'll make sure he's loyal to us."

Kirin ignored the gun in her face and turned toward Leo, who watched her intently.

"He's lying. The money's gone. I found it in the air ducts."

Leo's gaze casually switched from Kirin to Nicky and back. He stepped forward and motioned for Nicky to lower his gun. Nicky's face turned purple with rage. His body pitched forward like he was a step away from walking over and strangling her.

"Go on," Leo said to Kirin.

"I have proof. Your guys played Eminem—*Soldier* to be exact. Then somebody shot a hole through the ceiling into the air duct." Her voice shook, but she had their attention.

Leo turned. The man with the pistol nodded. When Leo turned back toward her, both thugs pointed their guns at her head.

Shit.

She'd now made herself enemy number one with both sides. She mustered every ounce of strength and kept talking.

"The money is hidden. Let the people I care about go free, and I'll give it to you.

Leo nodded, then pointed to the dark-haired woman holding Will and crooked a finger at her. She released Will and he darted to his mom, knocking into Nicky in the process—not so accidentally.

When he reached her, Will threw his arms around her neck. She kissed his cheek wishing her arms were free. She needed to hold her boy one more time. Kirin sobbed silently into his hair.

Leo cleared his throat and Will rose and glared at them. He wiped his mom's tears, then stood protectively next to her.

Leo spoke, "Money. Now."

When Kirin caught her breath, her voice shook, "What assurances do I have that they will go free?"

Leo smiled, "None."

Kirin glared back, "Then why would I? You'll never find the package in all the holes and nooks of this old house."

Nicky took two quick steps toward Kirin. He drew his pistol and placed the barrel on her forehead.

Will grabbed the arm with the gun to pull it away. Kirin screamed. For a split second, she envisioned Will being accidentally shot. Nicky struggled with her ten-year-old, who tenaciously held on to Nicky's arm like a bulldog attached to a steak.

When Nicky grabbed the gun with his other hand, he shook his arm and flung Will to the ground like a ragdoll. The thud of Will's head hitting the ground made her swear at the evil man. Like an angry animal she flailed around, pulling and ripping the skin on her wrists, writhing against the rope.

Sam dropped the charade and ran to Will's side. He placed a hand on her boy, then nodded to her as if to say, he's okay.

Kirin watched in slow motion horror as Nicky placed the gun in his right hand and alternated aiming from one target to the next and back. First Sam's head, then Will's. Over and over. Sam gave Kirin one last long look, mouthed, "I love you," and with tears in his eyes, laid his body across Will's to protect him.

At her strongest, she couldn't rip her hands free.

She was defenseless and either her child or her fiancé would die. She heard herself scream like she was not herself but an innocent bystander watching a movie.

This was all her fault. She'd gotten them into this. And she would never forgive herself.

Then…all at once, the room was silent.

It wasn't a surprise that a gun now rested at the back of Nicky's head.

What was surprising was the person on the other end of that gun.

Gianna's head spun in circles. She couldn't take it any longer. She didn't give two shits about Kirin, but her fucking old man would not be killing a kid today. He'd done enough damage to her—her whole life. The short troll grunted and put his hands in the air. Gun still attached. She grabbed it and flung it to the floor.

Thirty-nine years of pent up hostility toward this monster made her body quake. He'd been solely responsible for turning her into a whore. Nobody knew what he'd done to her real mother. She only had pictures of that woman. He'd treated his only child like a slave and sold her to the highest bidder—his brother Saul. If she really thought about it, she was glad Kirin killed that slime ball. He deserved it just as much as her father did.

Sam, who at first looked as if he was hatching a plan of his own, had not taken eyes off Kirin or Kirin's kid the entire time.

She watched him. His wavy hair and rugged good looks would make any woman want him.

Then it hit her.

It wasn't so much that she wanted *him*, as she wanted someone to connect with, and to share a normal life with. Someone who didn't judge her. She didn't *need* a man by her side to make her complete. But she wanted one. One that wouldn't decide she was a piece of crap, just because she was raised wrong. She wanted a good man like Sam.

Watching Kirin and Sam exchange gut-wrenching goodbye glances, she knew. Knew, no matter what she wanted for herself, she wanted him to be happy. Even if that meant he wouldn't be hers.

Nicky grunted, "Whoever you are, you just signed your own death warrant."

Shoulders back and exuding confidence, she spat, "You do not run this organization, you little hobbit, I do."

Nicky spun slow, arms raised and mouth open. A strange mixture of one-part respect and one-part rage, crossed his face.

"Don't do this. I've given you everything I had. You know I love you."

"*Love* me? You sold me to the highest bidder. Your own daughter. My mother ran out on me because of you." Gianna's voice shook.

Nicky's face turned beet red. "You're nothing but a slut and a whore with a law degree. A degree *I* paid for. I own you."

Gianna shook harder, then cocked the pistol back. In a sound no louder than a whisper, she said, "I'm so much more than that, dear father. I'm the Attorney who's gonna shut your organization down. Even if it takes my entire law firm and half the government to do it."

Nicky's eyes narrowed. He took two quick breaths and dove for the gun on the floor. When he did, he deliberately knocked her legs out from under her. Stunned, she scrambled up. Nicky's hot breath and murderous eyes were inches from Kirin's face, pointing the gun at Will and Sam lying on the floor.

Kirin screamed in his face.

Gianna did what any self-respecting, law-abiding citizen would do. She placed her body protectively in front of Will and Sam, raised her gun, closed her eyes, and squeezed the trigger.

The close range, deafening pop made Gianna's head pound. The top half of Nicola's body slumped onto Kirin's lap. As much as her father hated that woman, it was fitting that he died at her feet.

Gianna's mind sputtered as she stared at her father's cheap analog watch. It continued to move. Tick. Tick. Tick. Even after his body was motionless.

Joel grabbed Nicky's gun, shoved it in his waistband, and pushed Gianna's father's body off Kirin. Both Joel and Kirin's faces were splattered with blood.

After a long silence, Gianna spoke.

"A defendant, who claims he used deadly force to protect another, has to prove that he reasonably and honestly believed that the person he protected was in immediate danger of serious bodily harm or death and that deadly force was the only way to protect him or her from that danger. Furthermore, the defendant must also show that the protected person was not at fault for creating the situation and did not have a duty to leave or avoid the situation."

When she finished, she took a deep breath. It was over. Well, almost over. She turned and leveled a look at Kirin.

~*~

Uncontrollable shaking was Kirin's specialty. Her face was warm, wet, and sticky, as if someone had sprinkled hot, iron-smelling paint across her cheeks and forehead. She couldn't look away. The man who wanted her dead, lay at her feet. Blood pooled around his still angry face. When Joel tapped her, she snapped out of it and glanced up at him. She sucked in a quick breath. God, if she looked as bad as he did, she was glad Will was angled away from her.

"The money." Gianna spat, locking eyes with Kirin. As she said it, she shoved her gun back down the back of her dress pants.

Her hand still out toward Kirin, Gianna turned and spoke to Leo. "Consider this our gift. And an understanding that I have no connection nor a need to come after *you*. Nobody in this room does. Go in peace."

As most everyone turned toward Leo, Joel tucked the stack of cash under Kirin's hip.

Leo took one hand and smoothed down a ruffled spot on his perfectly white coat. He and Gianna eyed one another for several beats until Kirin cleared her throat.

Gianna cut her eyes toward Kirin, who lifted her hip, revealing the stack of cash.

Reaching down, she grabbed it and held it out, like a treat to a dog.

"I've had a change of heart," Leo smiled.

"How so?" As her eyes narrowed, Gianna pulled the cash back toward her body.

"Well, since Todd and Nicky are now gone, I think I'll merge this family into my own."

Gianna's voice was calm. Attorney calm. "We don't need a merger. We're no longer in business."

"Now, see…" He stalked toward her, "that just don't work for us. If you ain't in business, then who do I sell my product to and who do I get the girls from?"

"Law abiding citizens on the street, I imagine." Gianna's hand, wrapped around the cash, fell demurely to her side.

Leo narrowed his eyes, "You will hand over that money and you will obey me." Leo glanced around her. "That yo man?"

Gianna turned, "Not anymore. I don't need a man."

"Good. Then you don't mind if I kill him and the kid, right?" Leo pulled a pistol out of the pocket of his white fur coat and aimed it at Sam.

Kirin stood, hands still tied and screamed, "No! They're *my* family. Not hers. Please. I gave you the money. Stop!"

When she stood, Leo's thugs aimed their firearms at her head from across the room.

Leo clicked off the safety, gun still pointed at Sam's head, and stared at Gianna. He hadn't even acknowledged Kirin's plea.

Acting in tandem and with speed rivaling a gold medalist team, Joel, Sam, the woman who brought in Will, and one of the thugs with the bloody towel from the couch all overtook Leo. With four guns pointed at his head, his bodyguards moved toward them, aiming and yelling.

Stunned, Leo dropped his gun and froze. Gianna pulled hers out, took two steps forward and pressed her gun to his forehead. "I think I've proven here today, I can kill without hesitation. I suggest you order your dogs to lower their guns."

Leo gazed about the room, wide-eyed at first and then, like the switch of a light, casual. Gianna pressed it harder into his forehead. He raised his hands, slowly above his head. His look toward Gianna was a warning. "Okay. You win for *now*. Lower 'em.'"

"Boss, we got—"

"I *said*, lower 'em." The men complied, placing the guns on the floor in front of their feet.

Brandon, who'd been inside the room but lurking somewhere behind her, ran and gathered their firearms.

The thug from the couch with the bloody towel, turned and shouted out directions, "Alpha team, show our friends the way out."

Kirin spun.

She *knew* that voice.

Steve glanced back as the woman with the short hair and two other men in the room, plus Brandon, shoved the bodyguards out of the room.

Leo's jaw flexed and anger flashed across his face.

"We don't take a double-cross lightly."

Gianna spoke low into the man's face, "We don't take a bully lightly, either. I suggest you forget about this day and move along with your life. If not, I promise, my contacts in Washington would love to come down on every part of your business and destroy you. On that, you have my word."

Joel and Steve pulled Leo's hands behind his back and walked him out of the room. His eyes never left Gianna's as he nodded and repeated, "Okay. Okay. We'll see."

As soon as he was out of the room, Gianna's shoulders slumped several inches. She let out a ragged breath. Sam scooped up Will and held him.

Gianna tossed Leo's gun on Kirin's chair and made a swirling motion at Kirin with one finger. She complied. Swiftly, Gianna untied Kirin.

Kirin rubbed her wrists, then began using her sleeve to rub some of the blood off her face, but it wasn't working. She needed something better. Kirin spied Gianna's cream colored mid waist jacket and pointed to it, raising her eyebrows. Gianna followed her line of sight and answered, "Uh, no."

Gianna then took a quick look around, stepped over her father's body and bending over it, she spoke more to herself than Kirin, "He won't be needing this."

She pulled a clean, white hanky from Nicky's pocket and handed it to Kirin. The two women locked eyes. A silent understanding floated between them.

Kirin quickly wiped as much blood off her face as she could then looked to Gianna for approval. Gianna nodded. Kirin tossed the hanky and ran to Will.

He was awake and crying, rubbing his head. She knelt, using her body to shield Will from the gruesome sight behind her. She glanced over at Sam, who didn't even hide the fact that tears welled up in his eyes. Holding Will's head in his lap, he reached over, wrapped his fingers around the back of her neck and gently drew her to him. One tender kiss on the forehead told her everything she needed to know.

He was hers. Always had been.

Kirin pulled Will to her, squeezed him, and kissed his head, telling him they were safe. A horrified cry came from the opposite side of the room. Kirin looked up and followed Gianna's line of sight to Stacy. Her blank look had been replaced by a horrified one. She sat in the hardbacked chair and stared at the two dead bodies on the ground. To one of those people, she'd been married.

Kirin handed Will back to Sam and jumped to her feet, but Gianna got to Stacy first. Stacy stared from Gianna's face to the bodies and back. A surprisingly nurturing, calm voice came from Gianna as she untied her. When Stacy saw Kirin coming, she burst into tears.

Gianna stood, hands up as if to say she'd done all she could.

Kirin knelt and held her friend tight.

When she pulled Stacy back, she looked into her still wide eyes, "Told you we'd get through this." Stacy nodded and blinked back tears.

"Was my brother here?" Her teeth chattered.

"Yep. Mr. Perfect saved the day once again."

"Great. More to hold over my head."

Kirin looked over at Gianna talking to Will and Sam. Stacy followed her gaze. "Why is she being nice?"

She nodded as she glanced back at Stacy, "She saved us too."

Stacy shook her head as if that bit of information made no sense.

When Brandon came back into the room, he ran for Stacy, tearing off his suit jacket to cover her. Stacy tried to stand but wobbled and wound up sitting right back down. Brandon wrapped her in his coat and held her while she cried.

Steve passed Kirin as she was making her way back to Sam. He patted her on the shoulder and approached Gianna.

"Counselor. We need to call in these dead bodies."

Gianna scrubbed her face, looking disheveled for the first time in Kirin's memory. "You're right. You'll need to take me into custody since I killed one of 'em."

Steve nodded in agreement. When Gianna glanced up, it was like she was noticing him for the first time. She blinked a few times and their eyes locked. Steve's eyebrows shot up as a smile crept onto his face.

"You're not cuffing me." Gianna announced, sliding a pointed look at Steve.

"No?" Steve's expression was serious and all business, except the corners of his mouth. They curved upward. Kirin watched them. They were *flirting*. Talk about an odd couple...the criminal turned attorney with the all-American boy.

"No." Gianna answered. Now her turned up lips seemed to be betraying her.

"And you're not frisking me either." She announced, with a playful sparkle to her eyes.

"Wouldn't dream of it."

180

Chapter Thirty

Kirin had finally found Steve's kryptonite. Turned out you could glean precious information from the man when serving him warm scotch after a huge Thanksgiving meal. *Who knew?* Smooth scotch and buttery rolls made the Super FBI man spill his guts.

Steve admitted he'd put a transmitter in both Sam and Kirin's boots, knowing the other side would take one of them, if not both. Damn, but he was right.

His words were drawn out and slurry. But as Kirin walked into her living room carrying a tray filled with desserts, he lifted his glass.

"We all knew the girl could get into trouble, but who knew she could cook?"

With a tumbler of the warm liquid to his own lips, Sam raised his other hand. Her home smelled of turkey and dressing and family. But the permanent, just showered Sam smell had permeated the walls for good. She smiled down at him. God, she loved that man.

Joel walked into the room carrying one of his little tow-headed boys over one shoulder and his drink in his other hand. As he passed Sam's chair, he kicked his brother's foot. Sam leaned forward to not spill his drink and shot a playful glare at his brother.

"So, pinhead. Figure it out yet?" Joel said as he sat.

Steve shook his head, "No. Not this again. Just tell him already!"

Sam chewed on the inside of his lip. "Nope, I'm done. I don't care who hired you. I know Gianna did and Steve has denied it was him, so nope. Don't care. Just know that it takes your high-and-mighty-self down a notch or two knowing you were paid by both sides."

Everyone stared at Sam.

"*What*? That doesn't count. I was paid to *protect* Kirin, not do bad things."

Joel smiled, and then nodded toward Kirin, "You wanna tell him?"

Sam's gaze snapped to Kirin. "Wait…*you* know?"

Kirin nodded.

Sam's eyebrows knitted together as he shot a *WTF* look to his little brother.

Joel answered, "I like her better."

Kirin laid a hand on Sam's shoulder. "It was Kidd. The same man who helped me put all the pieces together that day at the Braves game, hired your little brother to watch over *you*."

Sam stared at her like she had three heads. Then turned slowly to stare at Joel, who nodded and began to explain, "Kirin's father paid you and made you promise to protect her, right?"

Sam nodded.

"He made his best friend Kidd promise to protect *both* of you. According to Kidd, you were the son Sonny never had."

Sam's face softened as his eyes misted over. Kirin kissed the top of his head as he watched his little brother piece it all together for him.

"And…" Joel continued, "Sonny wanted someone for his daughter who would not only protect her but help her trust and love again. So Kidd hired me to make sure you two get a happy ending to your story. Sonny was playing cupid before he died."

Sam sniffed and then took Kirin's hand and kissed it.

Steve pointed at Joel, "You know, your job isn't over yet, right?"

Joel took a sip, then nodded in agreement, "Not until they walk down the aisle, then it's up to them."

~*~

Stacy and Brandon sat at the dining room table playing cards with Will and Little Jack, while Dean, Kathy and Arthur talked in the kitchen. Her friend was still too thin and still emotionally beaten some days, but the smiles and good times seemed to be outweighing the bad. Brandon protected her like she was a crystal that would shatter if dropped.

Kirin walked past on her way back to the kitchen to refill her coffee and kissed her friend on the top of the head. Kirin was grateful that most of her family and friends were well and able to make it to the party.

All but a few.

~*~

Rosa sat stock still in a red booth with rips on the seat that pinched her legs if she moved. Her fists were balled under the table and her jaw ached from gritting her teeth. The diner smelled of bacon grease and strong coffee. She glared at the woman across the table. Angry wasn't even in her vocabulary. She was *furious*. Her own flesh and blood. *Named after her* for Pete's sake. One thing she knew for sure, the girl across the table had lost her mind if she thought for one moment she could forgive her for putting Will in danger.

And now…she wanted another favor.

What could be worse than putting Will in the same room as the Detroit Mafia?

She was about to find out…

~*~

Gianna put the finishing touches on the ornate bedroom. Purple lamp on the white table, sitting next to the new blue-toothed alarm clock that would charge her expensive phone and wake her up for the private school she'd enrolled her in. Pressed purple sheets and comforter lay flat with no wrinkles and matched the starched curtains. She stood back and wiped her brow. Purple had vomited in this room and as much as she hated the color, the girl—*her* girl, loved it.

Gianna grinned.

At twelve, she loved all things fluffy and comfy. Gianna had created a window seat, with shelves underneath stocked with every YA series she could find. And she'd had clothes ordered and delivered in her size. Gianna's personal assistant hung them all neatly on matching hangers. She'd even contemplated getting her a kitten.

Holy Jesus what had she become?

Her phone vibrated. She pulled it out of her pocket.

All was set.

If she was lucky, she might even come out of today with the girl's sister too.

Kirin recounted her terrifying time inside the mob house to Laura's unmoving body and closed eyes. She took the comb off her tray and straightened out her friend's hair. She was thankful they'd pulled her breathing tube out a few weeks before. Laura's doctors had told her husband Adam that the brain swelling had finally reduced and Laura was breathing on her own.

The only thing left to do was wait. But the longer it took for her to come out of the coma, the more chance she either wouldn't be herself or she wouldn't wake up.

It was Kirin's constant prayer to have her friend back.

The rhythmic beeping of her monitors had lulled the room, now decorated by her kids for Christmas, into a quiet slumber.

At the end of her daily visit, Kirin gathered her purse and leaned over to kiss her friend on the forehead when the strangest sound came out of Laura's chest.

It rumbled and sounded like a hunger pain. She glanced around. She'd had a feeding tube inserted several weeks ago. She found it ironic that Laura would be tickled with her new, tiny size.

The gargling noise rang out again, only louder this time. Kirin glanced at the heart monitor. It was elevated. Was she in pain. She tossed her purse back on the floor and grabbed up Laura's hand.

"Honey. If you're in pain squeeze my hand."

Nothing.

Then a gurgle again. This time, it sounded like… *"Kirin."*

Kirin held her breath, then yelled, "I'm here!"

Laura's mouth opened. Wispy whooshing sounds came out.

She lowered her face to Laura's mouth. Laura's eyes still weren't open.

She whispered back, "I'm here. What?"

Laura's eyes opened, wide and fearful. Kirin held her breath as tears formed in her eyes. She almost screamed.

"All my fault," Laura croaked out.

Kirin swiped at her eyes, kissed her friend on the head, then laughed.

"How could *anything* be your fault?"

"Were you hurt? They were after me, not you."

"Nobody is coming after you. You're safe. You're in our hospital. I have to run and get Adam and the kids." Kirin started to move when Laura grabbed her arm, digging her nails in. Her voice was desperate.

"You don't understand. Listen. The blast…it was my fault. They found out I was helping her…helping steal the girls and setting them free. Adam didn't even know."

Kirin stared at Laura.

"What girls?"

"The mob. They traffic them. I treated wounds and helped them escape. Todd's uncle, he found out…but he *couldn't* have known who our informant was…"

Laura was pulling at wires and crying full on now. Her medical team swooped into the room as one older nurse began pushing Kirin out the door.

"Nurse Lane, you know protocol…you need to leave," the woman grunted out as she guided Kirin backward.

"Kirin!" Laura yelled. Kirin fought against the woman pushing her, "I'm here!"

"Sam's not who you think he is!" Laura cried.

Then the door closed in Kirin's face.

The End

Preorder the third installment in the Kirin Lane Series coming Summer 2021.

Follow me for the latest news and giveaways:

Facebook:https://www.facebook.com/KelleyGriffinAuthor/
IG: https://www.instagram.com/kelleygriffinauthor
Goodreads:https://www.goodreads.com/author/list/991389.Kelley_Griffin
Amazon: https://www.amazon.com/Kelley-Griffin/e/B07V9T47D8?ref=sr_ntt_srch_lnk_2&qid=1590572512&sr=8-2
BookBub: https://www.bookbub.com/authors/kelley-griffin
Twitter: https://www.twitter.com/AuthorKTGriffin

Read an excerpt from Kelley's newest romantic comedy coming out Summer of 2021

Jen Harper Hates the *"f"* Word

Chapter One

Jen Harper was fightin' mad. And not just because it was five a.m., but because she'd just smashed her half-painted thumbnail with a frozen hammer trying to mend the hole in the chicken coop.

It was at the top of a long list of things that needed fixing at her new place on the outskirts of Knoxville. Ten days into January, and she'd already broken her New Year's resolution of no cussing not once, but twice. Screaming *"bad word"* just wasn't cutting it.

This wasn't supposed to be her life.

She should have been snuggled in behind her now ex-husband's warm back, dreaming of glorious vacations and her perfect children. She should have been sniffing the warm aroma of a freshly made pot of coffee and singing happy wake-up tunes like frickin Snow White. She should've had the perfect job, perfect husband, perfect body, perfect kids, and perfect life.

But she didn't.

If she was being honest, her mostly-perfect life was before. Before her company shut down. Before she and her co-workers turned close friends—those same close friends who got her through her six year old's cancer—all lost their jobs.

They were the ones who kept her from going batshit crazy when she found out about Tom's infidelity, too. Before the slim, blonde snake lured her husband out of their bed and into hers. Before her world came grinding to a halt. Her half-perfect life would always include those friends.

Sure. She wasn't the perfect mother and her body didn't look like it did when they were twenty. She got that. And she knew she wasn't completely innocent in the demise of her marriage. She'd take part of the blame right along with him. It hadn't been entirely his fault and she knew it.

Jen held tight to her thumb, squeezing the pain right out of it. She let out a frosty breath and brushed herself off, glancing up at the cold January sky. She vowed that today would be the day it would all turn around.

Today she'd nail the chicken coop *and* the new job interview. She could *feel* it. She was perfect for the Executive Administrative Assistant job at Colonial Construction Company or the *CCC* as it was known. And besides, she needed the job in the worst way.

She'd fallen in love with her house at first sight. Her first big purchase post Tom. An old Victorian. A hundred and ten year-old two story row house charmer with a slim staircase and oozing with character.

Too bad most of that "character" was falling down around her ears.

This was why she needed to nail this job.

The Wolfenbargers had owned the CCC since the 1920's. The largest residential building firm in Knoxville, they constructed everything from cookie cutter neighborhoods to mansions for the wealthy. They owned every part of the process from the bulldozer company that graded the land to the CCC Real Estate Company that advertised & marketed a new posh neighborhood. The company had been passed down from father to son since its inception.

Jake Wolfenbarger, or *Wolf* everybody called him, had been Jen's "it" guy in high school. He wasn't in the popular crowd or even on the football team, but he would've been the one she'd have chosen if she could've had her pick. And not because his family was loaded. She didn't even realize that in high school. He never drove flashy cars or wore expensive clothes. But because he was just a genuinely nice guy. Hot too.

They'd been paired up in Biology class for *one day*. That is until she'd embarrassed herself and had to move.

But even though his name was Wolf, he hadn't been a "wolf" at all. He wasn't a player or one of the thugs. He'd been nice. Nice to her anyway. Even a little after she embarrassed herself.

If social media could be trusted, he was still a bachelor having used all his time and resources to turn his father's struggling construction business into one of the most lucrative and busiest in town. He worked hard, but his posts seemed as though he couldn't remember how to relax or have fun.

Yes, she knew how demented it was that she'd stalked his profile and information, but she told herself it was what everyone did prior to applying for a corporate position. Never mind that she began stalking him the moment her marriage died.

After chucking her tools back in their pouch and inhaling her hot coffee to get warm, Jen changed into the best looking ensemble she had. A snug navy pants suit that flattered her everywhere. She'd not considered herself thin since high school, but she wasn't the "*f*" word either. She was curvy. Not bikini curvy, mind you, but heavy curvy. And this particular outfit always made her feel invincible and tall. Two things she clearly wasn't. Jen pulled her dark blonde hair into a low corporate pony and put on more makeup than she'd worn in years, highlighting her green eyes.

She ushered the kids out the door in record time. Another one of Tom's responsibilities when they were together, but she didn't mind this job at all. She loved torturing them by waking them up singing and acting crazy. Made her day when she was on the receiving end of eyerolls, slamming doors and huffs. And that was only from her fourteen year old.

But today, everyone seemed to know how stressed she was and nobody, except the escape artist chickens, gave her a hard time. And for once, everyone remembered to bring their weekend bags for dad's house.

As she drove into the parking lot, she took a deep breath. The only thing she'd held onto tighter than her almost-foreclosed house was her pride.

Inside her car, she spoke into her mirror. "You can do this. Shoulders back...remember names...don't look at the floor...chin up."

Jen took a deep breath and stepped outside.

The moment she entered the building, all that prep work and confidence flew out the window. She stopped cold.

No. Please no. Couldn't be.

Standing at the front desk was her nemesis. The *homewrecker.* The tall blonde leaned over a computer screen, listening yet looking bored as another woman explained how something worked. She hadn't looked up yet, which was a good thing.

Jen's body wouldn't move. It only took about ten seconds for people to start backing up behind her. She had to make her body go. Jen cleared the lump that formed in her throat. She'd believed Tom when he'd obviously lied about his mistress being possibly fired from the company.

Hell, that's the only reason Jen had applied for the job.

As soon as Jen moved, Ellis glanced up and froze. They must've looked like two competitive deer who'd just noticed each other as they were walking through the forest. At that moment, all the nasty things Jen had wanted to say to the wench, flew out the window. At least the ho had the decency to look apologetic.

Jen slowly shook her head as if to say how disappointed she was in the woman. She watched Ellis's eyes narrow.

Obviously, she didn't think she'd done anything wrong.

Chapter Two

"Wolf" Wolfenbarger needed only one thing, he thought, as he straightened his crooked yellow tie in the reflection of his monitor. He needed to ace his after lunch meeting with his mentor, Donald Garrett. Today was the day the ultra-conservative, pro-family man could choose to help him convince his Board of directors to back his proposal to build one of the largest subdivisions in all of Knoxville. It was a risk, but one he was itching to take.

This contract would pull his father's business out of the hole. It would mean hiring more staff, but also being outside all spring, summer and into the fall. Something Wolf craved.

As he tugged open the tie his little brother's wife had knotted for him and straightened it again, his mind reeled.

The only hitch was Mr. Garrett was a family man. One that had known Wolf since he was a kid. As the company's biggest stockholder, he'd been pressuring Wolf to find a life outside of work for years.

Only Wolf knew he couldn't do that to a woman. She'd be throwing away her chances and he knew it. It was part of the draw of dating Ellis. She'd never wanted kids. But Ellis was needy and narcissistic. He'd never felt fully connected to her and to be honest, it was scummy to date his assistant, no matter what she or anyone else said.

He stared around his office.

He'd still be in the dark if he hadn't walked in on them.

Wolf shook that image out. He'd already been thinking about breaking up with her. She just saved him the trouble.

And now, he needed a new assistant.

Walking out into his lobby, Wolf felt like he'd just blindly walked into a shit storm without a helmet. On one side was

Ellis, his freshly demoted assistant and on the other side of his lobby was the woman he was about to interview for Ellis's job.

Jen Cox. Well, Jen Cox Harper, now, although he wondered if she'd keep that last name.

She'd been the shy wallflower he'd been too much of a jack-tard to speak to in high school. When his HR director had brought him the stack of resumes, Jen's had been on top and for good reason.

She'd been at her last company for sixteen years until they closed the doors, which showed loyalty. She'd been an executive assistant which meant she could keep him in line, and she knew just about every computer program known to man. A definite plus since he'd spent the last fifteen years getting his father's company back on track and loathed being in front of a computer. It just wasn't his thing. Give him a hammer or a set of plans and he was happy. He didn't give two shits about stockholders and corporate meetings.

That's why he needed someone like her.

When he saw her, he knew exactly who she was. She hadn't changed much, although she looked more confident, more worldly. She still had that radiant smile from high school. She'd always impressed him back then with her witty comebacks when someone would call her short or height challenged. He'd loved her ability to fire back at the other idiots who didn't see her for what she was.

But today, he'd watched her walk in the door, exuding confidence like she owned the place. Until she spotted Ellis.

And now, if the daggers coming out of Jen's eyes were any indication, he'd need to step in and quick.

Wolf moved between the ladies, with his back toward Ellis. Jen's face changed immediately from angry to a full blown smile. A damn dazzling one at that.

"Ms. Harper?"

Jen's eyes widened in recognition and her face immediately turned pink. She swallowed hard and when she spoke, her voice cracked a bit.

"Yes."

Wolf grinned, "Would you care to follow me for your interview?"

His heart fell a bit when Jen looked around as if anyone would be a better candidate to interview her, than him.

"Uh...sorry, I thought I was here for the Executive Administrative job?"

"You are."

"But...I thought the job was for Mr. Hughes's assistant?"

Wolf motioned for Jen to follow him, but she didn't budge. Her feet were firmly planted, and her arms were crossed protectively over her body. Obviously, she wasn't going anywhere until she got an answer.

Wolf glanced over his shoulder. Ellis glared at the back of his head and listened in on every word. Great. Hash this out in the lobby. He bent so she could hear him and lowered his voice. "Actually the job *was* originally for his assistant, but that position has been filled by my old assistant. So now, the job is working for me. Will that be a problem?"

He watched as one eyebrow hitched up on Jen's face. "No... Gosh no. I mean...No sir, it'll be fine. I'd love to interview for your job...I mean for the admin job—for you…" Her downward gaze reminded him so much of the shy girl she was in high school. The one he really liked.

He couldn't stop his grin with a jackhammer.

"Good. Now can we go to my office?"

"Sure."

~*~

She must've pissed off her guardian angel to deserve this.

Seriously? She couldn't work for him *and* have a crush on him. This was insane. And how come the homewrecker still worked here?

Obviously, this was just another reason to tack on to the many, of why she couldn't trust Tom. He'd told her Ellis would be fired when the boss found out she'd had an affair. He'd been demoted—not fired—but only because they knew he had kids to support.

194

Everybody knew Wolf's parents had split because of his dad's many extra relationships. It'd tarnished his dad's reputation as a builder and lots of people wouldn't hire the company because of it. It was rumored that the only time Wolf's ill temper flared was when he found out about infidelity.

And exactly why did he have to have on a crisp white button down against his dark skin? And the tie. *Gah.*

All she'd ever seen him in were basketball sweats and t-shirts. She wasn't complaining. He'd looked good in them back in the day with his sandy blonde hair sticking out from under his ballcap and dimples that creased his cheeks whenever he laughed. He resembled a young movie star, all tan and white teethed. But a little shy at the same time. That's what drew her to him. He wasn't loud and obnoxious like most of the guys. He was quiet and witty.

And now, he looked regal and important. And *honest.*

Honesty, she realized, made him even more handsome.

Jen's hands trembled as she sat. Wolf walked around the large, mostly cleared desk and sat, too.

It was then that it hit her. Her husband and the ho had cheated on her right here in this office. *On this desk.* Jen started to shift uncomfortably. Her palms began to sweat. That same pain washed over her all over again and her face flushed.

Wolf watched her carefully.

"Are you okay?"

"Yes," she answered, then changed her mind. *Honesty.*

"No. No I'm not."

Wolf leaned forward. Concern etched his face. He nodded for her to continue.

"Why is *she* still here?"

Wolf took a deep breath. "My father. Mine and hers have been golf buddies since we were kids. It's why she got the job in the first place. I'm sorry. I know her being here hurts you, but my father is still on the board and he insisted."

Wolf looked at his shoes.

Jen straightened her shoulders and lifted her chin. No way in hell was she going to let the tears pooling in her eyes drop.

Wolf glanced back up and locked eyes with her. "If it makes a difference, you'd indirectly be her boss and you'd have my backing 100%. If she gets out of line at all, I can let her go. And..." he pointed at her, "I'm not hiring you because of the incident or to make her life worse, I'm hiring you because you were by far, the most qualified."

Her lips turned up despite her heartache. "Thank you." She said, and when his gaze settled on her eyes and didn't falter, she had to glance away.

Looking around the room, she wiped her eyes, then chuckled.

"What?" he asked.

"You don't spend much time here." She glanced around as she said it.

Wolf crossed his arms as a smile crept up his lips, "What makes you say that?"

Jen smiled back, "Well, first...there's a layer of dust on the computer."

Wolf stared down at it for a beat, then answered, "I hate 'em."

"And the picture frames on the bookshelf all have the pretend families in them. You know, the ones that come with the frame when you buy them?"

Wolf looked around then laughed at himself. "Okay, you got me. I hate this office."

"Can we do this somewhere else?" She asked.

His face brightened. "Can I buy ya lunch? I'm starved."

She thought for a moment. "I could go for some lunch, but I'll buy my own, okay?"

He narrowed his eyes at her like he was trying to work out a puzzle but nodded. "Café downstairs okay with you?"

She nodded. Wolf stood and walked around the desk.

Her brain had forgotten how he'd towered over her during high school. Maybe it was being married to Tom for so long. Tom hadn't been short, but he was no Shaq either. But most anyone next to her five foot frame seemed tall. Wolf was over six feet of tanned muscle from working outside. That hadn't changed since they were fifteen. He got his olive skin from his mama, who used to volunteer at their school. He must've gotten his dark, wavy hair from his father. Even his voice, deeper now than it was in high school, did things to her resolve.

This was gonna end badly.

Wolf walked past her and opened the door. The vacuum of the open door caused a whiff of his soap or aftershave or *buck lore* to float past her nose. She froze for a half second, nodded a thank you and sprinted through.

When she hit the button for the elevator, her fingers shook again.

What in the holy hell?

This felt like a first date with the President of the United States. Her mind sputtered. She randomly wished she would've shaved her legs.

What?

Where did that ridiculous thought come from? She shook her head at herself until she noticed him. He watched her as a smile played on his lips. Why did this feel so awkward? It felt like a first date.

When they exited the elevator and entered the cafeteria, Wolf got halted by one of his landscape designers with dirt stained gloves, holding two types of landscape rock. The young man spoke faster than an auctioneer. Jen smiled when Wolf shot her a "save me" look. She shook her head no and bit her lip. His eyes narrowed playfully.

The cafeteria was like an upscale version of a hospital cafeteria. It was clean, plenty of food to choose from, and smiling people standing behind each counter waiting to serve. She wondered if they smiled at her because she was with the boss or if they were naturally that happy to be at work.

When a janitor walked past, stopped, and ordered a burger, she watched these same workers fawn all over him like he was the King of England. Yep. They truly loved their jobs.

In fact, nobody seemed unhappy. From the workers to the staff coming in to eat...everyone seemed genuine and kind.

Tom had worked there for years on Wolf's sales force. He used to say the company was third in pleasantness, behind Chick-fil-a and Disney.

When auctioneer-boy stopped bending Wolf's ear, he joined her at the burger counter.

"So…what'll it be?"

"I'm thinking the grilled chicken salad?"

"Nope." He said as he took a step forward in line.

Jen stared at him for a beat, "Nope?"

He smiled down at her. "Nothing beats a burger at *CCC*. You do eat meat, right?"

"Yeah, but I was trying to go light."

"You gotta try one, I promise they're awesome. And you don't need to go light." As soon as the words came out of his mouth, his back straightened like a steel rod and his face turned beet red. His easy going lips flattened to a straight line.

"I'm so sorry. That was probably not the right…it was inappropriate…and I didn't mean it the way it…do you want to leave?"

She glanced up and smiled, "No. It's fine. It was nice. Thank you."

His shoulders lowered. When they got to the counter, he ordered two burger meals with drinks.

Hell. She'd continue the diet tomorrow for someone to say she didn't need to lose any of her baby pudge. Then again…the baby was eight. She needed to start calling a spade a spade.

Wine weight.

As they each carried a tray, Wolf nodded to the cashier, who nodded back. Then grinned at Jen as if he'd won the argument about paying for her meal. She shot him a look, like she'd get even.

Wolf pointed to a corner booth with his elbow and she nodded. Following behind him, she noticed little pockets of people eating lunch and talking. She stared outside through an expansive wall of windows and into a sleeping winter garden with a winterized fountain. Just from one glance you could tell it was well tended and would be beautiful in the spring.

Wolf stood at the table waiting for her. She could feel his eyes on her as she walked toward him. Two feet from the table and still ogling the garden, Jen tripped over the leg of a chair sticking out into the aisle. Her tray jostled and her drink catapulted forward. Were it not for Wolf's quick and expert hands, the drink would've hit the edge and exploded on his nice white shirt.

Thank God he caught it. Her face flushed hot. Her nerves were not only going to spill something on this poor man, *again*, but they were going to kill off this job interview if she didn't reign them in.

He took the tray out of her hands and placed it on the table with her drink. As soon as her hands were free, she held them to her eyes and shook her head.

He reached out and touched her arms to steady her.

"You okay?" he asked, leaning down.

"I'm sorry. You must think I'm the clumsiest person on the planet." Jen winced as she pulled her hand away from one eye to gauge his reaction.

Wolf grinned, "Wasn't your fault. And it was kind of a compliment to my garden," He motioned for her to sit before he did and then pointed out the window.

"Labor of love, right there."

Jen glanced back at the space and then to him. His eyes were bright and proud, like a new father.

"It's gonna be beautiful."

He smiled huge and dug into his fries, "I can't tell you how many boulders we've taken out of the ground in that space." He shook his head and smiled. "I was just trying to make it something nice to look at while our staff ate lunch and it's turned into this thing, with a huge price tag and a life of its own."

She stared at him for a beat. "You're good to your staff."

He swallowed and stared back, then gave her a half grin, "Thanks. Some of these loyal people have worked here since my grandfather owned it."

She nodded. Wolf dug into his burger and nodded for her to do the same. The twinkle in his eye, told her he forgave her and challenged her to take a huge bite.

Jen stared down at her plate. The burger looked like a frisbee. It took up most of the plate. She glanced over at her knife. No. She wasn't going to be prissy. For once, she was hungry. It didn't matter if she didn't look lady-like. He seemed to appreciate a woman, er—employee with an appetite.

When she glanced up at him, his eyebrows shot up and he shook his head no, like there was no way she could do it.

She was gonna look like a four year old with ketchup and mustard down her front, but she didn't care.

The new Jen would not be backing down from any challenges.

Wolf closed his eyes and took another huge bite all the way to the center of the burger. He hummed his appreciation.

Jen had to remind her jaw to close. Lord. She needed to check her hormones.

She shook her head and took in a mouthful. Automatically her eyes closed like his. The beef was perfect, and the mixture of white cheddar cheese, mushrooms and spices were unbelievable. She hadn't realized the moan that escaped was so loud, but when she opened her eyes, he stared at her with a look of wonder and something else. Something almost wanting.

Their eyes locked onto one another and she was instantly transported back to high school. Back where she'd embarrassed herself. And here she was doing it again.

She'd literally bitten off more than she could chew. He smiled big and she couldn't help herself but return it. She snatched up her napkin and held it to her mouth.

Okay, she'd taken too big of a bite. But no way was she gonna lose this challenge.

A round man with a white fluffy beard had silently sidled up to the table and watched them with a grin. They noticed him at the same time. Wolf wiped his mouth, then jumped up like someone bit him. He vigorously shook the old man's hand.

"Mr. Garrett!" Wolf's voice was higher and more formal than it'd been all morning.

Jen struggled to swallow the giant bite she'd taken, while beginning to scoot out of the booth.

The kind eyed older man watched her with a twinkle in his eye.

~*~

Damn. Of all the times for Mr. Garrett to show up, he picked now. The old coot was infamous for coming to a meeting early to look around. He wanted to notice how things ran when they weren't expecting him. Wolf knew this. But hell, the old guy was literally *hours* early.

"I wasn't expecting you until later today. It's so nice to have you here. Would you like to join us?" As he said this last part, he absentmindedly wiped a smudge of mustard off the side of Jen's mouth.

Jen had just swallowed the massive burger bite he'd dared her to take and stood. She'd stuck out her hand to introduce herself at the same time Wolf had wiped her mouth.

She'd frozen at Wolf's embarrassing lack of judgement and personal space.

Gah, he was such a dumbass.

Jen stared ahead wide eyed for a full beat before remembering herself, smiling and shaking Mr. Garrett's hand.

Immediately, Wolf's face flushed hot. He muttered, "Sorry," to Jen, then turned to Mr. Garrett, hoping he hadn't just witnessed it.

The old man just grinned. Of course he had. Mr. Garrett took Jen's hand in both of his and watched her but spoke to Wolf.

"So, my boy, I see you finally took that last talk we had to heart."

Wolf swallowed hard.

He had to give it to her. Jen had swallowed her bite, recovered, and smiled at Mr. Garrett, shaking his hand.

"Mr. Garrett, this is Jennifer Cox Harper. She and I—"

The old man interrupted, "I may be *old* Wolf, but I know exactly what you two are doing." He grinned big and released Jen's hand.

To her credit, she never faltered or even looked sideways at Wolf.

"And I'm here early to have a burger with your Dad, but as usual, he's late." Mr. Garrett looked around the cafeteria and then settled back on Jen's face. He motioned for the two of them to sit and then nodded graciously when Jen scooted over so he could sit with them for a moment.

"Miss Harper, please indulge an old romantic and tell me how you two met?"

Jen glanced at Wolf, raised one eyebrow and began, "Well, I was a sophomore at West where Wolf was a Junior. And I always got incredibly nervous around boys. So in Biology 1, I got paired up with *this* guy." She pointed at Wolf. He bit his lip.

Not that story. He'd been such an awkward ass. He'd liked her but had hesitated a moment too long to help her because his buddies would've ribbed him about it. When he finally decided it was the right thing to do, it was too late. If he could go back and smack that stupid kid on the head, he would.

Then again. He couldn't have made her a mom. Maybe things happen for a reason.

Jen continued, "Well, as I said, I got nervous around boys I liked, so I dropped a beaker full of solution on the floor. It busted and went all over his shoes. So I cleaned it up and moved to another table."

Mr. Garrett eyeballed Wolf. "I remember that kid when he was in high school. Pretty scared of what everyone thought of him. Son, I expect to introduce this beautiful young lady to Mrs. Garrett at our dinner party Saturday night."

Before Wolf could defend himself or even answer, his dad sidled up to the table next to him. Wolf glanced up to see his father's eyes rake Jen up and down. And for some damn reason it flew all over him.

"Hello, Father," Wolf said through gritted teeth, although the word "Father" sounded, even in his own ears, like a bad word. Wolf's dad's gaze snapped from Jen to him with a question in his eyes. Wolf glared up and met his father's stare.

As if he realized his error, his dad shook his head, then stared at the ground as he reached out and introduced himself.

Jen smiled at him, shook his hand kindly and studied Wolf. Great. He was sure she'd heard the rumors growing up about his dad's inability to keep his pants on with his own secretaries. He sure hoped Jen didn't think he'd follow in those footsteps.

Then again, he had with Ellis.

Mr. Garrett stood, brushed himself off and turned toward Jen.

Her eyes sparkled up at him. He reached down, took her hand, and kissed it, speaking at first to Wolf.

"Don't let her get away this time. Nice to meet you, Jen Cox Harper."

Jen grinned back, "Nice to meet you as well, Mr. Garrett and you, Mr. Wolfenbarger."

As the two men walked away and jabbered, Wolf watched her. She pondered on what was said for a beat, then bit back into her burger, raising her eyebrows as he had earlier.

She'd held her own with a man who owned most of their city. And he'd loved her. And she was polite even when his father faltered. She had confidence and was well spoken, even amidst the awkward conditions.

She'd do fine at CCC reining Ellis and the others in.

But something niggled at the back of his mind. Something that said, you can't date another assistant. Can't turn into your father. But he shoved it away.

She was perfect for this job and he'd be an idiot to ignore her twice.

The End

203